PRAISE FOR *LONG*

"[*Long Man's Pillow*] is gripping and thought-provoking. It elevates the genre and perception of 'cli-fi' as being more immediate and real than the usual focus on impossibilities. Vicki's experiences with a changing world are all too possible. This makes *Long Man's Pillow* an engaging attraction for readers who see the lasting effects of environmental change evolving in all kinds of community scenarios and individual experiences. Libraries and readers seeking compelling stories that juxtapose high-octane action with thought-provoking intrigue and character revelations will find *Long Man's Pillow* excels in a sense of realistic drama and life changes. This makes it perfect for book club and group discussion, as well as individual reader pursuit."

—Diane Donovan, Senior Reviewer, Midwest Book Review

"A gripping exploration of humanity's breaking point in the face of water scarcity, *Long Man's Pillow* is a page turner that will make you follow Vicky and her dog Gertie in the dry Apallachian mountains and lead you to essential discussions about life's fragility and the ethical quandaries that define us."

—Matcha, author of *Les Rencontres de Bombilo*, a French series about nature conservation.

"*Long Man's Pillow* is a strange name for a book—and for a river, as Julie Castillo's eco-futurist novel readily acknowledges. But the gripping tale she weaves of human nature in the face of water scarcity is all too familiar, and uncomfortable, a Parable of the Sower for our times."

—Erica Gies, author of *Water Always Wins*

THE LONG MAN'S PILLOW

Julie Castillo

Regal House Publishing

Published by
Regal House Publishing, LLC
Raleigh, NC 27605
All rights reserved

ISBN -13 (paperback): 9781646034512
ISBN -13 (epub): 9781646034529
Library of Congress Control Number: 2023943427

Cover images and design by © C. B. Royal

Regal House Publishing, LLC
https://regalhousepublishing.com

The following is a work of fiction created by the author. All names, individuals, characters, places, items, brands, events, etc. were either the product of the author or were used fictitiously. Any name, place, event, person, brand, or item, current or past, is entirely coincidental.

This story depicts the ingestion of such substances as sassafras, poison hemlock, and diphenhydramine (Benadryl.) These substances are known to be hazardous or, especially in the case of poison hemlock, deadly. The author does not condone their use and accepts no liability for the consequences of their ingestion.

Credit: The concepts of the "Long Man" and "going to water" come from the Cherokee people. The author is indebted to the authors and contributors of the Foxfire Books, from which she drew information and inspiration.

Printed in the United States of America

To Al, the center of my universe

1

I lie spread-eagled on a bare mattress in my apartment on Delaney Street at high noon, trying to get my head around what Mr. Rosen went through in his last few hours of life.

I close my eyes and bring his apartment up around me. The dusty light comes in zebra-striped from the broken blinds at the kitchen window. The reek of Pine Sol and yesterday's coffee. Weeks-old editions of the *Baltimore Sun* strewn across the countertop. Musty books stacked against the wall.

Plastic armrests. Pajama bottoms. The rumpled cushion of his wheelchair. His faded canvas bucket hat with "I Heart Jerusalem" on the front. I try to think his thoughts—*Jeopardy* on at five; where did I leave my prayer book, do I have enough jugs of water to last until tomorrow, and how many alley cats can I feed tonight before the landlord yells at me?

He's reaching out for something. A book, probably. The chair tips and skews out from under him. He cracks his left temple against the kitchen floor, enough to hurt like bejesus but not hard enough to knock him into merciful oblivion. So the coroner said.

He lies there with a left eye full of greasy linoleum and two legs that haven't worked in decades pinned under his chair.

He calls out for help that doesn't come until his throat runs dry. He struggles to pull himself free from a tangled mess of stiff legs, crusty blanket, and secondhand wheelchair so he can at least drag himself to the phone. He feels around for the one jug of water Vicki left nearby, but it's crushed somewhere under this mess of wheelchair, legs, and blanket. He struggles until he can't anymore. Then he just lies quietly and surrenders to the passing hours.

The shadows crawl up the walls and then it's night. His

tongue's become a lump of sand, swollen and sticking to the inside of his mouth. When he opens his eyes, a jab of pain makes him shut them again. What starts as a hammering ache at the back of his skull travels around his jaw and up his scalp. He lies there in the dark, parched and aching.

He hears footsteps around midnight and thinks, She'll come in to check on me and she'll find me here and set me upright and give me some water and it'll be all right.

He waits for her knock.

He dies sometime in the night. His teeth are gritted so hard against the pain in his head the coroner won't be able to pry them open in the morning. His last thought in this world is, Why didn't Vicki come to check on me?

Somebody's pounding on my door and I quit imagining I'm dead Mr. Rosen and become Vicki again.

"You still there? Girl, you better not have left without saying goodbye."

I'm up off the mattress and opening the door for Thora, who never waits until a door is properly opened before she's going through it. She fills my living room with the life it's been missing. All two hundred and seventy-eight pounds of her, round and meaty. When Thora's there, she's all there.

"The one time I didn't go check on him, Thora. *One time*! I thought, He'll be fine till morning."

She narrows her eyes at me. "Victoria Louise Truax, don't you go blaming yourself for that old man. He's not the first one to die in this damned dried-up city and he won't be the last."

"I had called a place. They were coming to get him in a couple of days."

"You know what I think? I think that old fella is lucky he's out of it. Sooner or later, the taps are just going to quit. And then the water trucks will stop showing up. And anybody who's still in the city by then is going to be in a world of hurt."

She tries my kitchen faucet. "Did you get any at all today?" A thin, rusty trickle patters into the cake bowl I use to catch whatever I can still squeeze out of the city's water system.

"It's been off and on," I tell her. "I'm trying to fill as many jugs as I can fit into the car."

"It's not too late to change your mind and come with us. Toronto's still got plenty of water."

Any second now, she's going to tell me I'm crazy for going to West Virginia. She's not wrong.

Her eyes rest on the packet from the lawyer, the one that arrived a few days ago, with a deed for a chunk of land belonging to an eighty-four-year-old Great Aunt Colleen I didn't know I had. On my dad's side of the family, which explains why I didn't know her. Now that I know I have a Great Aunt Colleen, I don't have her anymore, the lawyer's letter explains. But I do have seventy acres of forest and a cabin, on a mountain, outside of a town called Cooper's Forge, where she lived out the last of her days.

"That place is going to kill you. You know that, don't you?"

"Or it'll make me stronger. Isn't that what they used to say?"

"*They* used to say a lot of things, when *they* had enough water to live on."

"Maybe there's more to life than water?"

"This ain't no camping trip, girl. People are desperate. At least in the cities, they might keep rolling in the water trucks awhile. Out there, either you won't find anything to drink and you'll shrivel up like a raisin and die. Or you'll find water, and a bunch of assholes will jump you for it, and *then* you'll shrivel up like a raisin and die."

I slide a page of photos out of the packet. Trees. Shade. Cabin. Sunlight through wizened brown leaves that seem to cling to just the slightest flush of green. Or maybe it's my imagination. Baltimore hasn't seen anything green in more than a year.

"Jugs of water, anybody can steal, but this—" I press the photos into her hands. I've never owned anything this real before. "I'm not saying I'm going to stay. I just have to see it."

Thora looks through the photos of Great Aunt Colleen's place. She clicks her tongue. "If I thought I could talk you out of it…" She takes me by the shoulders and looks deep into my eyes. "Will I see you again in this life, baby girl?"

"If I ever get to Toronto, I'll find you."

She wraps me in a hug so full of tenderness that for a moment I wish I could just wear her around me like that, for the rest of my life.

Then she lets me go and I'm alone again. It's just me. My dead neighbor's silent apartment next door. The drip of the last of the municipal water into my cake bowl. And a piece of paper that's calling me to get in my car and drive west when every brain cell I have left is saying, Point that car north and floor it, if you want to live.

I got this ratty little Chevy from Hector, who owed me for some editing I did him a while back. He promised me it runs. And so far, it does. Whoever painted the thing this shade of monkey-vomit green deserves to be shot. But it'll do the trick. And it holds all my clothes, a few cardboard boxes of things I couldn't part with, a toolbox, a sleeping bag, two plastic milk crates of Ramen noodles, powdered milk, peanut butter, canned peaches, and forty-seven jugs of tea-colored water from a Baltimore kitchen faucet that isn't mine anymore.

I sit behind the wheel, the Chevy idling at the curb. I'm saying goodbye to the city that birthed me, where I spent the first thirty-eight of my years in this world. What parts of it are worth saying goodbye to? The little townhouse on Crofters Place, where Mom raised me? Lexington Market, where we'd go for crab cake sandwiches every Saturday? As a kid, I would goggle at the gape-mouthed catfish on ice and the skinned muskrats and squirrels gutted for frying. Good memories, those, but not the kind that need special goodbyes.

Maybe, for posterity, I should drive by the Bromo-Seltzer building, where Mom says she met my dad. The guy who was only part of my life for maybe the first year of it. I shake my head in disgust. Why would I want to go there?

I have only one detour to make before departing.

I drive away from my apartment on Delaney Street without looking back. I pull onto a quiet cobbled street and look up, three stories, to the balcony with the trellis of wisteria, two wrought-iron chairs, and a bistro table. A view that, with a limber enough neck, includes a slender rectangle of the harbor.

A severe red FORECLOSED sign swings from its balcony rail. Now that drinking water is getting rarer, the bank that took it won't be finding another buyer. A tiny one-bedroom condo with a harbor view. Quaint, historic, and once, nearly mine. Or half of it. The price of cutting short a messy divorce.

I squeeze my eyes shut against the stubborn gleam of a cloudless sky. *What are you holding on to, Vicki?*

Now, all I own is this green hooptie with a trunkful of cardboard boxes.

And seventy acres waiting for me on the side of a West Virginia mountain.

By two o'clock, I'm on my way. I leave town by that mess of spaghetti-like overpasses that dip and twist alongside the harbor. Or what's left of it. The harbor water wasn't fit to drink even before the rains stopped. Now, the water is choked with twigs, trash, and the corpses of rats.

I try to spot moonshiners. It's not illegal to dip water from the harbor, but it's a crime to sell it without a license. To sell it legally, they've got to guarantee it's filtered, distilled, purified—I'm not even sure what it takes to make that slop safe to drink. But with water in such short supply, you can bet the illegal water trade is thriving.

Outside the city, I pass mile after mile of dead lawns and dry trees. City parks and playgrounds, swings dangling empty. Kids don't play outside anymore. Dehydration's too risky. That's if there still are kids in these neighborhoods. I pass towns with broken windows and empty driveways; families gone north. It's what I expected to see. Still, I'm gulping back tears, passing by miles and miles of ruined lives.

I share the road with water trucks, military vehicles, and a few private souls like me, fleeing from the city. Or fleeing to it. Refuge is relative, I guess.

As I cross the counties of rural Maryland, I have less company on the road alongside me. I slow down to inspect a little blue Toyota abandoned half-in and half-out of the traffic lane. I puzzle over the reason the driver left it like that, not bothering to push it onto the shoulder.

A half-mile later, I see the driver himself. He's facedown in the gravel, his head turned toward passing traffic. A state patrol will be along in a day or two to collect, identify, and bury him.

I try not to think of Mr. Rosen.

The one good thing about not being able to drink all the water you want: you hardly ever need to stop and pee during a long car trip. But you do have to remember to drink your daily minimum. Better in small rations throughout the day. Under the shade of a stone bridge, I pull over to take a few sips from my thermos. I hold my nose as I drink. For the last few months, Baltimore's failing water supply has taken on a scent that reminds me of dead worms. On greasy pavement. After a rainstorm.

I lace my fingers over my head and stretch side to side to get the driving stiffness out, trying not to imagine what waits for me in Cooper's Forge. I promise myself for the umpteenth time I'm not going to ask anybody how Aunt Colleen was related to my dad. I don't care; I really don't care.

I coast down a hill toward a tall steel bridge into West Virginia. I study the trees on the other side of the river, willing them to be just a little less parched.

Midway across the bridge, I look down. What should have been a swift green flow is now a thick trickle in the center of mud flats.

Sunburned people in cutoffs and T-shirts troll what's left of the river in flat-bottom boats. They scoop the soupy river water into jerry cans. The West Virginia equivalent of moonshiners. It's midday and broiling hot, but I roll up the Chevy's windows against the river's stench. I hope to God they boil that crap before anyone drinks it.

The bridge pipes me straight into tiny Shepherdstown. A woman pushing a stroller waves to me from the sidewalk, the polite little five-fingered hand wiggle that, in the South, means, I don't know you, but hi, anyway.

I pass what must be a university campus. Tidy squares of lawn, pathways, neatly labeled classroom buildings. Except for the parched grass and the water trucks, I can't spot anything that would have been out of place before the rains stopped. Fewer people around than there should have been, but as I roll through the little college town, I see a sidewalk café with half a dozen college students seated at tables. A blue sedan passes me. Then an SUV with two golden retrievers lolling their tongues out the back window. The kinks in my shoulder muscles loosen, just a little. In this place, at least, something like normal life goes on.

After Shepherdstown, miles of rocky forest. The curled brown leaves clinging to the branches shake like maracas as I pass by. I spot a few small farms. Or the ghosts of farms. No crops grow in their fields. Tall blond weeds, right up to the front porches. Empty farmhouse windows remind me of the eyes of dead animals.

When the sun is just starting to melt behind the ridge of the mountains, I spot a sign with an arrow pointing to the right. It reads, *Cooper's Forge 27 Mi.* I make the turn. This road is smaller, rougher, and the trees with their clattering dry leaves press in closer. I've got the windows down, and as I drive, I become aware of a sound. It's everywhere. Like a thousand tiny dentist's drills, or the crackle of frayed electrical wires. It rises and falls. It jangles my nerves.

Cicadas.

It figures. All the cute wildlife is dying, but those demon-eyed bugs that make a racket fit to drive you mental, they're flourishing.

Mostly uphill now. This time I'm sure of it: the leaves are

a shade greener here. I come around a bend and see a gravel turn-off where two pickup trucks are parked. A woman and a man carry plastic jugs.

A patch of gray-green rock juts out of the woods, and in a cleft, I see a spot where they're slick and black with moisture. Moss sparkles on the rocks. At the base of the outcrop, a steady trickle is dribbling into the basins and jerry cans set all around. Half a dozen men and women fan themselves in the shade, waiting for their containers to fill. That's a lot of thirsty souls to quench from one tiny spring, but at least it's something.

That knot of doubt in my belly untwists a little more. I drive on.

On a particularly steep uphill my crappy little Chevy starts to hiss. It chugs like it's climbing up one wheel at a time. We make it to the top and I see what's probably Cooper's Forge in the valley down below. Even if my little green piece of shit gives out on me now, I can coast into town.

I pop the car in neutral and let it roll. The valley below is steep, less a valley than a canyon. A rusty railroad trestle spans the gap at the far end. Closer by, a rockface bears the faded words, *Chew Mail Pouch Tobacco.*

I tap the brakes as I roll into town, glancing around to get a look at my new neighborhood. Soon it will be too dark to see it well. Tin-roofed clapboard cottages sit alongside a creek bed. I can't see for sure, but the creek's probably dry. Some houses wear a skin of flaking tarpaper. Unless there's more to the town somewhere, Cooper's Forge is not likely to become the next vacation hot spot anytime soon.

A few of the yards are fenced in chain link. Apparently, people here coat their metal fences with silver paint when they get rusty. No one's out, but the town looks lived in. Gazing balls on the lawns. Cement roosters beside mailboxes. In one yard, I see a patch of garden with a few spindly tomato plants. In front of the only brick building in town sits a rusted green flatbed truck with a plastic tank on the back. Coasting by in the gloom, I can't tell if it's full or empty.

I'm running out of downhill, but I spot what looks like a gas station and a store. Two pumps and what might have once been a trailer, white paint with blue shutters, a narrow porch, and a sign that reads *Christmas Camping Supplies and General Store.* I can't figure out how Christmas goes together with camping. Maybe Christmas is the family's name?

I pull in and rattle across the gravel to the far end of the lot. The Chevy shudders to a stop, lurches, and dies in a fit of steam.

I take a moment. I'm listening over the din of the cicadas for the rush of water from the creek bed. Cicadas are all I hear. And the crunch of gravel underfoot.

I spin around. A lanky young white man in a straw hat and a lime-green T-shirt is waving at me as he approaches. His shirt reads, *Rock Climbers: We're Getting a Little Boulder.*

"Overheated," he says, in a not-unfriendly tone. "Happens a lot on these hills. Mind if I take a look?"

"Thank you." I pop the hood for him.

I get out and stand with him while he lifts my hood. He wears the kind of desperately scraggly beard young guys grow to make themselves look older; it's the same rusty-red as his ponytail. He smells like old sweat, pork n' beans, and citronella.

"Ah, here you go. Hose's come off." He whips out a green bandana and uses it like an oven mitt to poke around in the steaming black guts of my car. He reconnects something to something. "All-righty. Once it cools down, you want to top off the radiator, and she should be good to go."

"Thank you so much, but I think I've got to where I was headed, if this is Cooper's Forge." I extend my hand. "I'm Vicki Truax. From Baltimore."

He breaks into a broad grin, takes my hand, and pumps it.

"Vicki Truax from Baltimore? Cool Breeze."

I blink at him. There's no breeze in Cooper's Forge, cool or otherwise. Maybe that's his way of saying he likes my name. Or my city.

"Breeze for short."

Ah, okay. It's his name. "Nice to meet you. Breeze."

"You're coming to Cooper's Forge, you say?"

"Yes, actually. I just inherited a house and some land."

"Oh my. Are you related to Miss Colleen?"

Is that a good thing or a bad thing? I try to gauge from his face. "Yes. That's right. Although I actually don't remember meeting her."

"You moving out here with family, or is it just you?"

"Just me."

"No husband?"

"Divorced."

He grins again, a smile so wide I'm wondering if it's going to end up in his ears. Nobody smiles like that in Baltimore.

"Well, Vicki Truax. Salutations! Let's get you fixed up for tonight and then tomorrow I'll introduce you around. Come on in the store a minute." He gestures for me to follow him, and I do. "I'd let you stay in the house tonight, but Bright doesn't care too much for strangers."

Breeze leads me to the screen door on the front of his shop and holds it open for me. I'm halfway through it and picking up the scent of bananas and tomatoes, intermingling with raw meat that I'm not sure I'd call edible. Except for the deep woods all around it, this place would transport me back to the corner shop on Caroline Avenue I remember Mama taking me to when I was a kid.

"Look at this, babe!" Breeze calls out. "I went out for the mail and came back with Colleen Bolivar's next of kin."

A slender woman in overalls rises from a chair behind the counter. She glances toward the back room like she's thinking of making a run for it. Then she changes her mind and comes out from behind the counter. For a flicker of a moment, she looks up at me with eyes that remind me of blue China teacups, then she drops her gaze.

I extend a hand. "Hello, I'm Vicki."

She takes a step back and looks at my hand like it's covered in mouse turds.

"Vicki, this is my wife, Bright. This is her family's camp store."

That would make her full name, Bright...Christmas? Or maybe she didn't fancy keeping her maiden name and she's Bright Breeze. Whatever she is, she's already making for the back door, murmuring a "nice to meet you" that makes me think it was anything but nice.

"Shy." Cool Breeze shrugs.

He gathers some things from the shelves and fixes me up with a pup tent in the gravel lot behind the store. He sets a folding chair in front of a gray coil mounted on a wire frame, which he hooks up to a car battery. "We don't do flames, Vicki Truax, not with everything as dry as it is."

He pops the lid off a can of beef stew and sets it over the coil, which begins to glow cherry-red. "This doodad was invented by Cindy Lyons, our very own resident genius. All of twelve years old. Take it up to the cabin with you tomorrow if you like."

He presses the warmed can of stew into my hands.

"You need any water?"

"No, I'm good. Thanks."

"'Righty, then. Just unhook that lead right there from the battery when you're done."

They climb into a brick-red motor home that looks like it's sat behind the store for a few years. Bright gives me a sidelong glance before she shuts the door. I'm pretty sure I hear a lock clicking.

I linger in the camp chair just long enough to be polite, as the night creeps up and swallows the last of the light. God, it's dark in this valley. The sparse golden rectangles of light from nearby houses don't do anything to lighten the gloom. I try hard not to look at those windows; if folks are watching me from inside, I don't want to know.

I never get into the tent. I can't shake the desire for locked doors between me and this place I don't know. I end up sharing the backseat with my boxes of clothes. I wrap a towel around my head to muffle the screech of the cicadas. Once I'm locked in for the night and using my bathrobe for a pillow, I remember I didn't get any water out of the trunk in case I need it during the night. I'm more creeped out than thirsty, so I stay put. I go back to dreaming I'm Mr. Rosen, with my dry tongue stuck to the roof of my mouth.

☙

I wake to tapping on my car window and there's Breeze, holding a tin mug of coffee and waving. I drink it down and he says, "Whenever you're ready, I'll take you around to meet the neighbors."

"I think for right now I just need to go up and see my land."

Breeze blinks at me a long moment. "Okay. Folks around here respect privacy, that's for sure. But," he jerks a thumb at my dilapidated Chevy, "Ol' Bessie here isn't going to get you all the way up there. Not on those roads. I'll run you up in the ATV."

An hour later, we're headed up a mountain track on the machine equivalent of a bucking bronco, all my worldly possessions following behind in a trailer. I swear Breeze is aiming for every bump he sees. Any second now, my stuff is going to be launched off the side of this mountain.

The longer we ride, the more I'm convinced just how right Thora was. I came all this way to die.

And then, all at once, we're there.

Breeze hits the brakes in front of a tiny log building with a slanted porch. He commences taking my boxes of stuff out of the trailer and setting them on the ground. Something in the trailer catches his eye. He looks at me sidelong. Then he lifts out a long, thin object wrapped in an olive-green woolen army blanket. He hesitates, toeing the leafy dirt.

"So, um, my neighbor, Early, brought this around for you

last night. With you bein' up here by your lonesome, maybe it's not such a bad idea."

Breeze holds the bundle out to me.

I unwrap the blanket and find a double-barreled shotgun, with a cardboard box of shells rubber-banded to the stock. I slide a fingertip along the cold metal barrels and down the polished wood. A shudder runs up my arm.

"I hate guns," I tell Breeze.

"Figured as much," he sighs. "I'm not big on 'em myself."

I rewrap it, shells and all, and hand it back. "Please tell Mister...Early I do appreciate it, though."

"I'll be up to check on you later. Or somebody will. We all did it for Colleen; we're happy to do it for you too." He aims another ear-splitting grin my way. "Welcome home, Vicki Truax. Enjoy!"

And then he's off, buzzing away down the mountain.

I'm standing frozen until the last of the motor noise dies away. The silence is so thick, it's almost a physical thing, like cotton I could reach up and pull out of my ears.

And then, a bird sings.

City girl that I am, I have no idea what kind of creature I'm hearing. But its song is like clear, cold water splashing out of a crystal pitcher. The bird chortles out its tune in little bursts: clear trickling song, then silence. A few seconds later, another burst of song. Each time, the tune is different. But in the same bright, bell-clear cadence.

I give over all my attention to the silver melody of this little bird. And as minutes pass, my heart calms, my vision clears, and I'm ready to have a look around.

The drought has left its mark: many of the tallest trees stand naked and dead; more than a few have toppled over. But there's more life all around me than I've seen in far too long. The morning light coming through the foliage is the color of lemon-drops, of emeralds.

I open the door of the tiny building and walk into the place my aunt Colleen called home. A waft of cool, shadow-damp air brings me the scents of grease, ash, and old blanket. A bed with a thick wooden frame and a pile of green, yellow, and lavender quilts in one corner. A chair with a cane seat and an apple crate in the other corner. The apple crate is draped with a doily. A stone hearth and fireplace take up one end of the room.

Two sensations nestle in my heart at the very same time. If I were to put words to them, they'd be, *Sweet Jesus, how could anyone live like this?* And, *Where has this been all my life?*

2

I'm like a mama with a newborn baby. I want to know every inch of this perfect thing that is mine.

I start with the cabin. I put my hands on everything. The cast-iron pot with a lid and four little feet that sits on the stone hearth: greasy, gritty. The long garlands of dry string beans that hang to one side of the fireplace: brittle, fuzzy. Two shelves of canned meats, sticky with a film of greasy fireplace soot. Two more shelves of Mason jars filled with murky maybe-vegetables. Cool and smooth. A heavy cloth-wrapped thing that smells like rawhide, hanging in the darkest corner, which turns out to be a cured ham with a thick white rind. A knife sticks in the side and a hunk has been sawed off one end.

Aunt Colleen has only one trunk of personal belongings. Knitted shawls and sweaters, carefully wrapped in brown paper. No knickknacks. One framed photo: a middle-aged couple, arm in arm. The man's about to give the woman a big fat smooch. None of the usual scribbles on the back or edge of the photo to give me any clues about who's in the picture.

Then I'm outside in the quiet lemon-drops of sunlight that polka-dot the leafy ground. I'm fingering the logs of the cabin. The saw-marks on the wood. The crumbly matter that fills the cracks between the logs. A stack of firewood in a rack with a tarpaper roof sits to one side. An empty chicken coop backs up to one side of the cabin, a little wire run alongside is still full of brown and white droppings and tufts of white fluff.

Holy hell, I could have chickens. Thora would laugh her ass off.

I run leathery leaves between my fingers. All these plants and trees are strangers to me; I don't know the names of any of them. I'm going to have to get my hands on some field guides. I need to be on intimate terms with everything that grows here.

Something on the ground catches my eye half a second before I'm about to step on it. It's a feather. A big one. Long, brown and white striped. Hawk? Eagle? Might as well be pterodactyl for all I know. I run it between my fingers; the vanes make a zipping sound when they snap back into place, like taffeta. I close my eyes and run the feather through my fingers again. I tuck it into my back pocket.

As soon as my eyes close, my ears open. A bird shouts a three-note call from somewhere over my left shoulder, then, far off in front of me, another bird responds. Just beneath this conversation, other birds trill and warble, ask and answer. Leaves rustle, even though there is no wind. The woods make no noises at random; even the softest whisper speaks volumes. This whole forest is talking to itself. And I'm going to learn to speak its language.

I walk a spiral outward from the cabin, in larger and larger circles. Aunt Colleen's cabin and yard sit on a tiny patch of level ground. Everywhere else, it's steep and rocky, steeper as I travel downward from the cabin.

The afternoon is getting old and I'm still exploring. The lemon-drops of light have turned to long, dusty shafts. I'm walking the edge of a steep drop off. This is probably the end of Aunt Colleen's property and the beginning of someone else's. A few feet beyond the toes of my sneakers, the ground falls away into a steep ravine. I tiptoe closer to the edge, probing with my foot to see if the ground will hold me. The knot of roots and dry grass at the cliff edge feels solid enough. I slide as close to the edge as I dare and look down.

The cliff face is a jumble of rusty red and black stones and twisted steel. Girders, catwalks. The remains of a shed. A broken concrete slab. And on it, what I can only guess was once a water tower. Plates of metal riveted together to form a huge bowl, like a giant witch's cauldron. It once stood on metal supports, but it now rests against the cliff face, its legs buckled and broken. It might have been painted a bright robin's-egg blue one time, but its paint job is now just a whisper of faded color, washed over with long fantails of rust. Its roof is off. The shallow cone that must have covered it lies beside it, turned upward to the sky. Inside the upturned roof, there's a powdery red coating. The dusty corpse of water. Two metal trash cans on chains lie at the bottom of the cone.

I get it. Someone was using the roof of the water tower as a cistern. Nobody would go to the trouble of doing that if they had a perfectly good way to fill a water tower. When the water source that filled the tower ran empty, they knocked the roof off it and used it to catch rainwater. They scooped water into the trash cans and pulled them up by the chains, like buckets in a well.

And then the rains stopped coming.

A shudder starts at the base of my neck and works its way down into the pit of my stomach. The story in front of me is being told across the Eastern Seaboard, from Florida to Maine, in a hundred different chapters, in a thousand plot lines. In cities and in the middle of nowhere. All through our childhoods, and half our adult lives, we never had to spare a thought for it. But all you need to do to ruin a person, a neighborhood, or a nation, is take away their water.

I need to see what's left of the water tower. I balance my way carefully along the edge to where I can almost see inside the tank itself. I lean out, sticking one arm behind me to counterbalance.

The roots and stones beneath me give way.

One moment I'm teetering and windmilling, the next I'm falling out into nothing. I think, *Land on your feet, Vicki, then collapse on your side.* I twist my body to try to hit feet-first, but I don't. I strike the inside wall of the water tank with my right shoulder and I bounce. I land deep in the bowl of the tank, and then I'm rolling.

The inside of the tank is full of rust chips and hard, dried mud. As I careen toward the bottom, I'm coating myself in it. When I finally come to a stop, I'm facedown in a pile of leaves and twigs. I see sunlight. I'm staring through cracks where the tank broke against the cliff side when it fell. I'm lying on a lattice of rust that's probably not going to hold me for long.

I wait for my head to stop spinning and the ringing in my ears to die down. I try moving my left arm. Stiff, but intact. Then my right arm. So far so good.

I ease up onto my knees and crawl away from the rusted cracks. I brace myself against the wall of the tank and ease my way up until I'm standing. I take inventory. Head spinning. Getting a goose egg on my right temple. I'm bleeding from the shoulder that hit the side of the tank. I'm wobbly, but nothing's broken. As far as I can tell.

I press my back to the side of the tank and slide down to sit. My head pounds. I close my eyes and rest against the tank, wishing I could go back to Baltimore just so Thora can kick my ass for this.

Once the world stops spinning, I take inventory of my surroundings. How to get out? I expect there's a ladder somewhere. How could there not be a ladder?

I become aware of the sound of something motorized, on the cliff overhead. It's getting closer. Then a man appears at the cliff edge.

"Are you hurt?"

"I don't think so. Just stuck."

He disappears. A moment later, a tail of blue and orange nylon rope appears. Then he reappears, feet first, in a blue climbing harness, zipping his way down into the tank. In a moment, he's standing at the bottom of the tank, helping me to my feet.

He's in a red and white polo shirt that somehow just doesn't match his surroundings. He's wearing a black helmet and carrying a second one on a clip at his side.

"This old thing's a safety hazard. I keep meaning to have it demolished. I'm Steen. Steen McMasters. Your neighbor."

He offers his hand and I take it. He squeezes, hard enough to startle me.

"I'm Vicki—"

"Yeah, I know." He hands me the spare helmet, loops some

harness around me, then shows me how to use the rope to hoist myself up the side of the tank.

Once we've clambered our way back onto the cliff edge, he unhooks my harness and says, "Let me drive you over to the clinic in Elkins."

"No, really, I think I'm okay."

"Sure? Well, let me give you a chance to get cleaned up, at least. My house isn't far."

I was raised, like all city kids, on the ultimate mom commandment, the one about not taking rides from strangers. But I'm thinking there must have been a caveat in there for those occasions when you've just been fished out of a broken water tower.

He helps me over to a shiny red quad runner that looks like something out of a sci-fi movie. I climb on behind him, and we're buzzing away, up a trail that crisscrosses the side of the mountain.

We come to the top of a ridge, and a wooded glade opens before us, a little scoop out of the mountainside. A tall metal fence encloses a tile-roofed yellow stucco house that is about at home in a West Virginia woods as champagne in a paper cup. I count three outbuildings painted in the same butter yellow as the house.

My neighbor stops the quad before a heavy metal gate, which rattles open obediently. He follows my glance and smiles. "That's my well house. My bottling shed. My delivery trucks."

He gestures to three gleaming white panel vans, each with a logo of an aquamarine water droplet with the white silhouette of Cooper's Mountain in the middle.

"So, you're in the water business?"

"Licensed and bonded. The real deal. I can get a hundred and twenty dollars a gallon because it's pure mountain water. In the cities, everyone gets their ration off the government trucks for things like bathing and laundry. But those who have the means, they buy mine for drinking. So long as people still have money, water's worth more than fine wine."

"And so that's what the people down in the town are drinking? Your water?"

"Aw, hell no. Nobody in Cooper's Forge has that kind of money."

"Then what do they drink?"

He gives me a look I can't quite read. "Come on. Why don't you take a hot shower while I get your clothes cleaned."

"A hot—what?"

He breaks into a grin. Then he leads me inside the stucco house through an echoing foyer and into a tall-ceilinged great room with a stone hearth the size of a small school bus.

He leaves the room and comes back holding a fluffy white towel and a midnight blue bathrobe. He leads me down a hallway and opens a door to a room that might as well have led to another world. This bathroom is nearly the size of my old apartment: white and gray marble, silver trim, and a shower that could easily hold four people.

"Stay in as long as you like. And then come sit by the fire until your clothes are ready."

The door clicks shut. I crank the shower knob full on and a blast of water leaps from the shower head. In seconds, it's so hot I can barely stand it. I strip out of my rusty clothes, open the door just enough to hand them off to Steen, then I climb into the first real shower I've had in almost two years.

The scalding hot water pounds my skin and all at once I'm sobbing. I plunge my face into the torrent to try to get hold of myself, but now I've let something loose from deep inside of me and it's not going back in. I stand there for what could be hours, blubbing into the shower stream.

Toweling off afterward is almost as delicious. I'm like a snake that's just shed its skin.

There's a knock at the door and Steen's voice comes through, muffled. "I'm leaving some stuff for you to clean your cuts with."

I stand naked in front of a tall bathroom mirror, turning this way and that, finding wounds I didn't know I had, swabbing them with peroxide and taping them over with Band-Aids.

Later, I'm clean, dry, bandaged, wrapped in the dark blue bathrobe, and making my way shyly toward the main room, and the huge stone fireplace, where he's got half a tree blazing away. Cool Breeze's words from yesterday swim up to the surface of my mind. Something about how we don't make fires on the mountain on account of the drought.

He motions for me to sit beside him at the hearth, and when I do, he grins and hands me a crystal glass full of clear liquid and ice. "We've fixed up your outsides. This will take care of your insides."

I bring the glass up to my nose. Something herbal, floral, and very, very alcoholic. I take a tiny sip. It's fire, ice, and lemons, with a hint of thyme. It burns all the way down to my stomach, where the warmth spreads out like a tiny nuclear reactor.

"My bathtub gin. I make a batch twice a year. What do you think?"

His voice has a musical fruitiness to it, like he's selling me something. A super-sweet breakfast cereal, maybe.

"You make this? Here?"

"With the water from my well. Pure Appalachian spring water, right out of the heart of the mountain. The best in the world."

"Okay, this is going to sound ignorant as sin, but the water that fed that tower has run out, right? And you live above it. And water obeys gravity. How can you have water?"

"Not to get too technical, but what's underneath us right now is called a karst aquifer. They can form even high up inside mountains. Neat little pocket carved out of the limestone, still full of rainwater it's been collecting for thousands of years. It won't last forever, but for now, there's still plenty to drink in this mountain. I have the only well up here that's still producing. Every drop of water in this mountain belongs to me."

He tops my glass from a crystal decanter. We sip our gin. I stare into the fire. Something's not adding up.

"So, you've got the only water. You've got lots of it. And you're not giving any to the folks in town?"

Steen's mouth tightens a little. He regards me, just a beat longer than politeness allows.

"Look, Vicki. You're a long way from Baltimore. Don't overestimate these people out here. I know how charming they can be, but the simple truth is, they don't understand a whole hell of a lot about the way the world works. The world you and I come from."

I glance around at his museum-sized living room. "You and I don't come from the same world."

"No? You understand what it means to own something. Otherwise, you wouldn't be up here on this lonesome-ass mountain, checking on property that, three months ago, you didn't even know you had."

A little knot of anger draws tight between my eyes. If this fool is going to lecture me, he'd have been better off leaving me in that tank. "And your point is?"

"Well, there's this thing called eminent domain, it's when—"

"I know what eminent domain is."

"Okay, well, those yahoos in town are trying to use it to get control of my land, take over my well. And it's my only source of income."

He pauses, as if to let that news sink in. "And if they can do it to me, they'll come after you next. So, if you think about it, it's lucky we bumped into each other today, huh? I'm good for more than just fishing foolhardy young ladies out of water tanks. Sooner or later, you're going to need me on your side."

"I just got here yesterday. It's a little soon for me to be picking sides."

He sets down his glass. "Let me go check on your clothes."

He leaves the room and comes back with my clean, warm clothes in a bundle. I take them into the bathroom, still steamy from my forever-shower, and I get dressed, taking as long as I dare.

When I come back out, he's standing near the front door, smiling again.

"So, feeling better?"

"Lots. Thanks."

"Then let's get you home."

I step out of his house and into a night full of bug sounds. I'm going to need to whittle myself a pair of ear plugs.

He zips me back to Aunt Colleen's cabin and pulls up in the yard. I step off the machine gingerly, trying not to bump my sore spots. He turns and grabs my wrist in the darkness.

"This lifestyle's not for everybody, Vicki. You're enjoying the novelty of it for now, playing mountain woman. But pretty soon, the fun wears off. When that happens, when you decide you want out, you come see me."

He throttles up the quad and rides away. I watch his two red taillights snaking away up the mountain until they disappear.

I'm in pitch black. I wave my hand in front of my face. I can't see the cabin. I can't see anything. I turn around and walk toward where I think it is, waving both hands in front of me like I'm doing the breaststroke through this bug-filled swimming pool of darkness.

My fingertips find the porch rail, then the door, then I'm inside, with the door closed, crawling under Aunt Colleen's quilts, and drawing up into a fetal position. My bruises throb. I find a few tears left over from my shower and I cry them onto the pillow.

It might as well be a rock concert going on out there. Crickets jangle, cicadas drill, and who-knows-what goes slithering through the brush. All. Night. Long.

I lie there, sleepless, with my eyes open to the blackness and my ears full of sound, until a tiny patch of sky outside the window turns a shade of indigo. Then I settle into a thick, dreamless sleep, as though I'm sinking into a deep, cool well, down and down, deeper than the last memory of light.

৵

It's late morning before I'm anywhere near awake.

My ears are working long before my brain cares what they're hearing. It's something like the thrum of a motor, tickling me awake. Getting louder, then stopping. Footsteps rustling in leaves. Then the creak of weight on Aunt Colleen's front porch. Something heavy dropped there with a thud. Creak of footsteps stepping off the porch.

My mind finally snaps to work and says, Vicki, footsteps mean you got a visitor.

I tell my body to get up out of bed, but the minute I move, my muscles shout back.

As I lie there, willing myself to try again, the porch creaks a second time. Another heavy thud and a metallic rattle.

Now I'm up and limping stiffly to the door. I open it, expecting to thank Steen, or Cool Breeze, for whatever they've just brought me.

Only it's not either of them.

This man is climbing aboard a tiny scooter without looking back, and he's already gunning his way out of my yard. He's got white hair in a long ponytail, a floppy wide-brimmed hat, and a jean jacket.

He's left a pile of supplies on my front porch: two jerry cans, two apple crates, the topmost of which is full of food cans, and a tin pail filled with what looks like straw. I pull away a handful of the straw and find six perfect brown eggs.

I call out, "Thank you!" to his retreating back.

He doesn't turn around. He makes a gesture with his left hand that seems to say, It's nothing. Or it could mean, Back off, lady. Then he's riding away, up the mountain, leaving a little trail of blue smoke as he goes.

Inside the second crate are a flashlight and a pack of batteries, a sack of flour, a tin canister of cooking oil, and a Mason jar of ground coffee.

I've got exploring to do, neighbors to meet, and mysteries to solve. But first, I'm going to celebrate my escape from the water tower with breakfast in my new home.

I lug in the battery-and-coil contraption and set it up in the hearth. I take down a heavy jet-black skillet from a hook in the wall and place it on the coil. I pour oil into it. I saw off a shamefully huge hunk from the hanging ham and lay it in the pan. It sizzles and quivers like a living thing; it gives off an aroma of brown sugar and leather.

I crack two eggs into the pan and watch their twin orange orbs jiggle in the sizzling oil. I find a tin pot, give it a quick rinse, fill it, add some coffee grounds, and set it alongside the pan.

The scent of frying ham and eggs overwhelms my senses so completely, I forget about the stiffness in my shoulder and the stinging of my cuts.

I crack and beat one of the remaining eggs in a chipped blue bowl, add flour and water, and pour the mix alongside the frying meat and eggs. I don't know what I think I'm making. Whatever it is, it puffs up into a bubbly glob and turns crispy brown at the edges.

I drag Aunt Colleen's cane-bottom chair outside into the sunshine and set the apple crate alongside it. I dish out my slab of ham, fried eggs, and bread onto a tin plate. I strain the gritty coffee through one of my clean T-shirts and pour it into a mug.

I sit in hazy sunshine, surrounded by a carnival of green and gold, serenaded by the clear warbling of unseen birds, and I dine like a queen.

I've never lived in a place that was mine.

My home. My land. I'm the empress of all I survey.

Stiffly, I move around the cabin and yard, setting up my new life. I discover just how many life-forms share this place with me.

In the pocket of Aunt Colleen's green housecoat, hanging on a peg by the door, I discover a family of newborn mice nestling, pink and squirming, in a bed of soft grass and fluff. In my apartment on Delaney Street, rodents meant setting traps and calling the landlord to send in an exterminator. But in this place, the mice were here before me. I can't just evict them.

I pick a bundle of sweet-smelling herbs growing by the porch. I'm standing on Aunt Colleen's cane-bottom chair, tying them to a rafter, when I see two gleaming black eyes staring down at me. They're on a long rigid stalk of a neck, underscored by a mirthless grimace of a mouth. Shiny black scales on top. Powdery gray scales below. Something ancient in me chills me to a dead stop long before my mind finds the word *snake*.

I tumble off the chair and back away. I've never seen one in person. Not even at the zoo; you couldn't pay me to set foot in a reptile house. I search my mind for a file marked Snake Knowledge, but I come up empty.

It's not taking its beady eyes off me, so I won't look away either, not for one second. I fumble around me for any kind of an object that might discourage the thing from dropping down from the rafter and coming at me. My hand finds something long and metal on top of the kitchen table and I grab it up and hold it out in front of me like a sword. It's a wire egg whisk.

That's right, snake. You come near me, prepare to be scrambled.

The snake retreats. I follow its movement, needing to know where it ends up. God forbid the thing would crawl into bed with me tonight. Do they do that? The animal winds its way along the rafter and then disappears through a hole in the eaves. I'm still shuddering an hour later.

In late afternoon, I lie on Aunt Colleen's bed and watch a double line of ants travel up and down the wall from the floorboards to a crack under the windowsill. I watch for a long time before I discover that the ants in the outbound line carry tiny chunks of something; the ones in the inbound line carry nothing.

What happens if I create a traffic jam? I press a fingertip to the wall right in the middle of their highway. Both lanes halt. They throw up their feelers as though surprised. They turn to the ants nearest them and waggle feelers at each other. And then, as though they've come to some unanimous decision, they bypass my finger to the left and go about their mission.

I try counting the ants. They won't stay still long enough for me. The ones I see must be just a tiny sampling of the number that live in the hive. Nest. Whatever ants live in. Then I try counting the number of different birds I can hear. Then the number of cicadas. I puzzle through impossible calculations, working out the sheer number of living things that call this mountain home. Bugs, birds, snakes, and now me.

Evening shadows rise. I don't know why everyone talks about night falling. It doesn't. *Daylight* falls, night *rises*. And here, if you lie still long enough, you can watch it happen.

The next thing I know, I'm startling awake in pitch-black-ness. Someone is in the cabin. I can't see him but every cell in my body knows a person is standing, motionless, in the dark-ness. I jump out of bed on the far side. At least there's a piece of furniture between him and me. Why in God's name did I refuse that gun?

I grab for my flashlight and struggle to find the on-switch with my trembling fingers. He bolts out the door. I turn the flashlight on and aim it at his retreating back.

A hot spike of anger hits me between the shoulder blades. Your mountain, Vicki. Your home.

All at once I'm leaping over the bed and chasing after him. The intruder hurtles into the dark brush, fleeing down the mountain. I thrash along after him, trying to keep him in the beam of my flashlight. I lose him.

I pick my way back to the cabin. My flashlight beam falls on my two jerry cans, now emptied of their precious contents and tossed into the yard. The flour tin lies empty too: a powdery white coating scattered on the leaves. The last of the brown eggs are crushed into a sticky goo of spattered yolks and bro-ken shells.

Stealing my food and water I can halfway understand. That's need. But he didn't steal it; he ruined it. That's a message.

I'm standing in the dark, in the woods on the side of a mountain, with all my means of survival seeping into the ground around me, and the nearest person I trust is a thousand miles away in Toronto.

I've done a fair amount of living in thirty-eight years, but nothing has prepared me for this. I think about picking my way through the darkness to Steen McMasters' house. But I'm much more likely to get my ass lost than to find my way there. And who knows if the jerk who just paid me a visit is out there still, lying in wait.

Even in a parched mid-August, the mountain gets cold at night. I shake off my numbness, get myself inside the cabin, and this time, I draw the bolt. I pick up Aunt Colleen's wrought-iron fire poker and sit on the edge of the bed, tensing at every sound.

I'm out of my depth. I can't possibly live like this.

❦

It's late morning before I'm anything close to conscious again. I don't have the slightest memory of falling asleep, but I'm curled up in the middle of Aunt Colleen's bed, still clutching the fire poker. I drag myself to my feet and open the door.

The jerry cans and flour tin are gone. Two new, full containers of water sit on my porch, along with a mailbox-sized brown paper sack full of something hard and lumpy.

I tear open the top of the paper sack and scoop out a handful of foul-smelling brown pellets. Either my benefactor thinks I have a dog, or he's under the impression I'm desperate for protein.

The sound of an approaching motor puts me back on alert. An ATV is zigzagging its way up the mountain toward me. When the rider comes in sight, I catch a flash of red hair and a lime-green T-shirt and I go limp with relief.

Cool Breeze pulls up in front of me, breaks into an ear-splitting grin, and says, "Salutations, Miss Vicki. I've come to fetch you to a picnic. In your honor."

"Hey, Breeze. I had an intruder last night—"

"I know. We'll talk about it after lunch. You okay?"

"I'm…still a little shook up."

"Why don't you go get cleaned up a little and I'll take you

down to Althea's. You'll feel better after a home-cooked meal."

Moments later, we're buzzing down the mountain and into Cooper's Forge. Breeze takes a sharp left at a red mailbox flanked with an antique plow painted school-bus yellow and entwined with bright columbine.

We bump down a dirt driveway, kicking rooster tails of red dust as we go, and pull up in the yard of a pale blue two-story clapboard house. A willow tree the size of a barn weeps long tendrils onto the lawn. Its leaves are parched and curled at the edges, but still mostly green.

Under the willow, I can make out a long table with a checkered tablecloth, and at least a dozen people sitting around it. Some of them are waving.

Breeze dismounts and windmills his arm toward the group under the willow. "Come on. Let me introduce you around." I follow him under the drape of half-dry branches.

Inside the willow fronds, it's like a curtained pavilion. The table is decked with platters of fried chicken, bowls of coleslaw, plates of biscuits, and blue-enameled pots loaded with buttery corn on the cob. Sweating pitchers of iced tea stand at intervals along the table.

The folks at the table range from barely adult to elder. They're dressed in clean collar shirts, jeans, blouses, sundresses, and crisp cotton shorts. Some of the younger ones are waving and smiling at me, saying, "Hey, there, Miss Vicki!" and "Welcome, honey!"

I quickly scan up and down the table for a man with a white ponytail. Nobody sitting here looks anything like the stranger who's been leaving gifts on my porch. But then, I did only see him from the back.

Kindly eyes meet my gaze up and down the table. Mostly. One gray-haired fellow with no neck is staring straight at me, the corners of his mouth turned down so far they might as well be stapled to his shirt collar. Ex-military. I don't know how I know that. Definitely none too pleased at the audacity of my existence.

I turn my gaze to the friendlier faces.

At the far end of the table, the place of honor, sits a large woman in a green and white gingham sundress, with a thick silver braid slung over one shoulder. Her arms remain crossed over her bosom. Her eyes travel over me. She doesn't smile.

Breeze takes me by the arm and leads me up the table. "Vicki, meet Mack and Tippy, those two girls, Becky and Cindy, are theirs." Tall, lank, and angular, Tippy looks like he was born to play Bob Cratchit. Never wandering far from his side, Mack could be his Mrs. Cratchit. "And that's their son, Rennie." He gestures toward a coltish teenager romping with a pack of kids. "Then there's Carl, and Tom and Susan, Miss Lila…" I try to hang on to each name as he introduces me, though I forget each one instantly.

"This here's Mister Roland Early Slade." He gestures to the man with the stapled-on grimace. This mass of bad news sent me a gun to protect myself?

"And of course, you've already met my sweetie." Breeze gestures to the overall-clad young woman I met at the store on my first day. Bright Christmas nods at me without a whisper of a smile.

"And here's Aunt Althea." Breeze brings me to stand before the grand woman with the braid. "Her and your aunt Colleen were friends for, I don't know, bunch of years."

Althea rises from her chair, grasps my jaw, and turns my face this way and that. Her touch is rough but kind, a combination as odd as apple pie and hard cheese, and somehow, just as satisfying. I'm her prize heifer and her beloved daughter, all at the same time.

"Colleen's in your eyes," she says, still studying me. "You're not as dainty as you look. You got what it takes to weather that mountain?"

"I hope so."

They seat me at the other end of the long table. They load a China plate with enough chicken, biscuits, beans, corn, and slaw to feed three of me, and place it in my hands.

As I'm tucking into my plate of food, I notice a silver-framed photograph, crowned with black-eyed Susans, propped up against a sugar bowl. In the photo is the same woman from the picture in Aunt Colleen's trunk, the one getting smooched.

"You probably don't remember her," says a slight wisp of a woman with long dark hair and high cheekbones. She has bright, quick eyes, like the eyes of the pet ferret my friend Alice had in high school. "Colleen talked of you. Lila, and Althea, and Carl and Early over there, they remember when you and your mama came to visit."

"I was here?"

"Just the once, as far as I know. You were just a tiny thing."

"Miss Colleen, she was postmistress of Cooper's Forge for nigh on thirty-seven years," says a wrinkled woman a few seats down. I search my mind for the name Breeze told me just moments ago. Lila, maybe.

"She was an educated lady, like you," the dark-haired woman says. "She brightened up more than a few dim bulbs around here."

"I'd never have learned no math a-tall without her, I swear to God," says a meaty blond man to her left.

The dark-haired woman offers me her hand. "I'm Susan, and this is my husband, Tom. I can tell by the way you put your words together, you've got college, Miss Vicki. I wonder, once you get settled in, would you take on few students now and then?"

"Well, I don't know if I'm really qualified."

"In our eyes, honey, you've got all the qualifications you need. Would you come down on Fridays to Miss Althea's house, tutor up a few kids, and stay for supper? Just whenever you have the time."

"Of course," I say, "I'd be honored." To myself, I think, I'll just say yes until I can get my affairs in order and hightail it for Toronto.

The heavyset silver-haired man to my left extends a hand to me. He has a ruddy, bulbous face like a potato. "How do, Miss

Vicki. I'm Carl. I live on the far side of the creek bed from you. In the winter when the leaves are down, you can see my place from your one."

I fumble to set down my pile of food and take his hand. It's fleshy and calloused. Soft but hard.

"I understand you had a bit of a to-do last night."

"Someone came into my cabin and emptied out my water jugs." I swallow the quiver that's trying to creep into my voice.

The table falls silent.

"That shouldn't have happened to you, Miss Vicki," Tom says. "Especially not when you've just got here. We'll take care of it."

"I'm sorry, take care of what?"

The folks around the table exchange uneasy glances.

"They're trying to scare her off, is what they're doing," Early says. His voice matches his face: grim, disapproving.

"With that land occupied, it makes it harder for them to stake a claim, if they were to find something," says Susan.

"Who are we talking about, exactly?"

"Moonshiners, Miss Vicki."

"People know this mountain's got water, it's not like we can hide that fact. Sometimes we get moonshiners. You know what them are?"

"Yes. We have moonshiners in the city too. People selling contraband water."

"Your piece of land sits over top one of the earliest coal shafts in the country. The water pipes the miners put in served Cooper's Forge for over a hundred years. That's all done now."

"There ain't but two good springs up there these days. That don't stop moonshiners from trying to tap the mountain wherever they can."

"Two springs? Isn't it only one?"

"You all hear?" Carl bellows to the folks at the table. "She's here hardly more than a day and the rat-bag's already got to her." He turns back to me. "So, you met that city fellow lives up there, on the piece of land next to your one."

"Steen. Yes, I met him."

From the far end of the table, Althea addresses me in a slow, measured tone. "Now, listen, honey. That fellow ever comes around trying to cut some kind of deal with you, you just tell him good night. Hear?"

"You probably already know about the Kelso Springs, Miss Vicki—"

"The what?"

"So, as you were coming into town, right at the bottom of the creek bed, you see an old driveway with a chain across it, two stone posts on either side?"

"I might have."

"Until fifty or so years ago, that was a fancy spa for rich folk. Built after the coal miners left town, with water from the aquifer the miners piped into. Shut down when the mines' aquifer tapped out. Been rotting out there for longer than anyone in town can remember."

"I got an album up the house," says Althea, rising stiffly. She stumps off toward a screen door off one side of her porch.

"Of course, as you can imagine there's people who swear the place is full of haints. All kinds of stories been going around for a long time. It's a chore keeping our teenagers from getting in trouble out there."

"Don't go anywhere near it, Miss Vicki. It ain't safe." Susan squeezes my hand. "There's people staying up in there that don't belong."

Something about the way she says this makes the hair on the back of my neck prickle. "People?"

"Outsiders. Moonshiners. Crooks. We don't know 'em, we didn't invite 'em, and they ain't welcome."

"Sometimes moonshiners come in there and hide up in the Springs, and then they raid the mountain at night."

"Now and again, a bunch of us get together and rout 'em out. We'll go tonight and send 'em packing."

"Okay," I say meekly. Should I thank them? Should I offer to go with them?

Althea returns with a red leatherbound photo album which she plops on the table beside my plate, flips the pages, and presses a forefinger against a postcard picture. "There," she says. "That's what Kelso Springs was like when it was the fashionable place to go."

The postcard is from a time when photos were hand-colored with hues not found in nature. In the picture, a stately three-story building gleams in the sun, bright white with forest-green trim, resplendent with balconies. To each side of the main building are what appear to be rows of dormitories, smaller copies of the big hotel. Turquoise pools fed by waterfalls flash at the feet of the proud buildings. Stern white statuary flanks the pools. Bright carnivals of salmon-colored roses edge every patch of lawn.

The place overflows with life. Fashionably dressed young couples smile and wave from white wicker chairs on the lawns. Yellow parasols and long white gloves. Checkered sweater vests and slicked-back hair. All these happy, wealthy people, so alive at this one moment the photographer squeezed off his flash. Every one of them now worm food.

"It's beautiful," I say quietly.

"Not no more, it ain't."

The conversation lulls long enough for my eyes to drift around Althea's yard. A gaggle of kids sit at a table of their own, doing their darnedest to make a mess of their Sunday outfits. I smile at their teasing and snorting. The tall teenager, the one Breeze introduced as Rennie, sits with them on a too-small chair. He's holding two chicken legs, making them dance. The kids fall over each other, laughing.

I'm so caught up with their merriment, it takes me a while to notice the two huge guys sitting together on a wrought-iron swing some distance apart. They don't give impressions of being overly bright. They sit picking at plates of food on their laps. Their round, bearded, man-baby faces wear long pouts, like they've just been spanked. They remind me, just a little, of the pudgy twins from *Alice in Wonderland.* I stifle a giggle.

One of them, with no neck and a spiky yellow buzz cut, looks up at me as though he's felt my eyes on him. He stares at me. Something awful is in that gaze. Like he's not looking at a human being but at a rock, or a trash can. While he's staring, he pulls a MoonPie from his pocket, unwraps it, and shoves it whole into his mouth.

Tom follows my gaze. "Them's Bill and Newt Pike. Cooper's Forge boys, but only just. Grandsons of a fellow who died a few years ago. They work for your neighbor, the one who's stealing our water."

"Sorry, I'm confused. He told me he owned the well."

"Oh, I'm for certain he's got a deed and all that. Deed is a piece of paper that means something, in ordinary times. But in case you hadn't noticed, Miss Vicki, this whole part of the country is dying."

"Well yeah, the thought did occur to me."

Susan says, "It ain't rained in Cooper's Forge in nineteen months."

"Baltimore hasn't seen rain in almost as long."

"Now, any old shithouse lawyer would say, he bought the land; he holds the deed. By that way of thinking, the water's his. But I ask you, Miss Vicki, is water some pretty little luxury?"

I open my mouth to reply, but Tom answers for me. "No, it ain't. Water is a matter of life and death. Ain't no man has that right, to cut off the means of life from his fellow man."

Early slaps the table three times with his open palm. I jump in my seat, but the folks around him are nodding his way. Maybe that's how he shows approval.

"If it were up to Steen, you'd be sitting round this table with a bunch of skeletons right now."

"So, then, it's not Steen that's leaving me water and food."

"That fellow, he wouldn't give a drop of water to a dying man," says Carl.

"Then who's been taking care of me?"

"That'd be Alaric."

"He's a strange old guy. Not a native. Lives just the other side of the ridge from you. Keeps to himself, though."

"He comes around in the morning couple times a week and drops a trailer with a full water tank outside the church. Done it since our wells quit. Won't take nothing for it, neither. Kept your aunt Colleen in water too, when it got harder for her to come down the mountain." ·

"I should thank him."

"We've tried. Best just to let him be."

"Some folks are like that, especially around here."

"Something about that mountain draws people who'd rather live alone," Althea says as she stirs a crock of barbeque beans with a long-handled wooden spoon. The flesh under her arm flows along with the movement, like a thick custard. "You and Colleen are of the same kind."

By the time the last chicken bone has been picked clean, the final blush of sunset is dimming above the ridge of the mountain and the cicadas are in full voice.

I shake hands all around. Susan, the bright-eyed woman, takes both my hands in hers and says, "Stay, Miss Vicki. It'll get easier, I promise. Please stay."

More than one of the townsfolk invites me to sleep at their house for the night. I politely decline; I'll never know exactly why. Maybe because I can't have it both ways. I can't remain the tough mountain woman in their eyes and still hide out on a neighbor's couch while someone's up there ransacking my land.

Althea surprises me with a warm hug. Then I climb aboard Cool Breeze's ATV and we're away, down the driveway, onto the road, and up the mountain track.

For the second time in three days, I climb off an ATV and let it drive away, leaving me alone in pitch blackness. Alone with a million cicadas, a snake and, quite possibly, a stranger lurking in the bushes nearby, waiting for an opportunity to do me harm.

3

I'm not asleep.

I sit on the edge of Aunt Colleen's bed, rigid as a flagpole, my eyes wide open but seeing nothing, my ears straining to hear through the clamor of insects.

I've lost my sense of time. My watch is no help; the battery died yesterday. The bloodless chill in my fingers and toes tells me it's well into the deepest part of the night. It could be one o'clock; it might just as well be five. I wouldn't know.

I've been bracing so long to hear a human sound that when it does come it chills me through. It begins as a series of slow, dull thuds, something heavy striking the earth. Then a hiss and a thud, like a shovel driving into rocky ground, rhythmically. Then silence.

I will myself to stand, grab the first heavy thing my hand falls on, ease the cabin door open, and sidle out into the night.

The shoveling and thudding has started up again. I place one foot in front of me, toe around in the darkness until I'm sure of my footing, then ease my weight onto that foot. Doing this, I discover, lets me move through the night without making a sound.

I see lights flickering through the brush downhill and to my right. I ease along in the darkness, one foot following the other. I'm not myself. The Vicki Truax I know is far too much of a coward to do what I'm doing. The sensible Vicki thinks things through. Whoever I am now isn't even sure of what she's going to do next.

I can see them now: two guys, muscular and young-ish. One is holding a pickaxe and staring around him into the darkness while the other drives a long-handled shovel into the side of my mountain, tossing shovelfuls of rocks and dirt behind him into the night. He pauses to wipe his brow and his companion takes over, attacking the rocks with his pickaxe.

I move closer. I'm no more than a city bus's length away from them now.

Some noise behind them causes them to startle. They drop their tools, grab up their flashlights, and aim the beams into the night. They mumble something I can't hear. I wonder why they're so twitchy.

In a moment, they pick up their tools and begin again to chip away at my mountain.

This is the stupidest thing I've ever done. They've got heavy metal tools; they could even have guns. What have I got? An iron fire poker.

At last, my brain begins to thaw. I ease my way silently, back up the hill to my cabin. Once I'm inside, I turn on the flashlight and set it back on the table, lighting the peg beside the door where I hung my bag. I dig around it until my fingers touch the cold aluminum cylinder of the mini-airhorn I kept handy during those nights back in Baltimore in case I ran into trouble coming home from work after midnight.

I turn off the flashlight and slip softly back into the night.

You're crazy, Vicki, I tell myself.

I creep onto the rocks over their heads, as close to the two digging men as I possibly can get. I kneel and aim the device's tiny plastic trumpet toward them. I breathe. Then I jam both thumbs onto the button.

The blast of sound shatters the night. I keep the button squeezed until every puff of air has been launched from the can.

Once my ears stop ringing, silence drops in on me like a wet blanket. For a blessed moment, the cicadas have stopped. So has the digging. I make out shuffling noises below, the clang of dropped shovels. Then a pair of footsteps, thudding away down the hill.

I clamber to my feet and make my way over to the edge of the hill. I see two flashlight beams bobbing through the darkness, as the two diggers run headlong into the night. I examine the little air-horn, now emptied of its canned air. This worked? Hell yeah, it worked.

A fierce pleasure leaps up in my chest.

Vicki Truax, mountain lioness. Defending her territory.

❧

I spend the rest of the night sitting in Aunt Colleen's cane-bottom chair with her quilt and her cast-iron skillet across my knees. I plan to stay awake until daylight.

It's not that I don't hear the buzzing of the dirt bike coming up my drive; it's that I'm in such a heavy stupor by early morning that it's like the sound is coming from another driveway, in another town, across a deep ocean, on a far-off island.

I'm fighting for consciousness, swimming toward its shore, but fatigue keeps pulling me back. As if from endless miles away, I hear footsteps on my porch, the thud of jerry cans set down, then the drone of the dirt bike fading away down the mountain.

Sleep pulls me under again.

When I finally break free of its undertow, it's because there's an unexpected sound coming from my porch. A musical two-note whimper.

When the sound finally registers in my foggy brain, I sit bolt upright in the chair. I wait for it. It comes again. That two-note cry, so full of loneliness it's as if my heart's going to split.

I fumble for the door and throw it open.

There's something new on my porch, and it's gazing up at me with two big brown eyes beneath a wrinkly brow. It's chestnut brown except for black ears, which hang like twin velvet drapes from the sides of its head. Its paws are big enough for a dog twice its size.

I catch sight of a note tied to the rope around the pup's neck: *This is Gertie. Treat her good. Keep her with you on a leash for a week. After that she'll never leave you.*

"Gertie?"

At the sound of her name, she leaps to her feet. I suppose all dogs wag their tails, but this one's entire body breaks into a wiggle so vigorous, it nearly knocks her off her feet. The moment her eyes meet mine, she tips her head back and commences a joyful yodeling: "*Yo, Yoooooouuu! Yo, Yoooooouuu!*"

I kneel and try to pet her head, but her tongue is faster. She's licking all up and down my arm. I pull back instinctively, which throws me off balance. She seizes this moment to come at me with her two big forepaws, and she knocks me backward onto my ass. Now she can reach my face. I throw up my arms to ward off the torrent of dog-slobber, but I can't help giggling, which the pup takes as a sign of approval.

I have a dog. Vicki Truax. From Delaney Street. Has a Dog.

ஓ

Gertie!

Those soulful eyes. Clunky paws. Rumpled lips. The way she looks at me ruefully, with her wrinkled brow and saggy eyelids. That glance that says, Oh, Vicki. How *could* you?

I open my boxes and show her my stuff. My complete collection of Toni Morrison novels in hardcover. My black jeans with the rhinestone angel on the back pocket. Photo albums. Relics from a life that was mine a week ago but now is fast becoming ancient history.

She touches her nose to each item, then looks up at me for an explanation. I describe each thing to her. What it is. What it's for. The story of how it came into my life. The reason this particular object made it all the way up a West Virginia mountain in a cardboard box when so many other artifacts from my thirty-eight years of living got left behind without another thought.

Gertie hangs on every word.

Her arrival changes the equation in ways my heart and gut understand but my mind has yet to work out. The impossible image of me showing up at Thora's tiny Toronto apartment with a dog that's easily going to outweigh me in a matter of months. The far more impossible notion of giving her back to my mysterious benefactor.

Gertie's had the indoor tour; now I want to show her our land. From the lawyer's packet of documents, I fish out a surveyor's map. I smooth it flat on the kitchen table and examine the contours of the mountain, and the little symbols that stand for survey markers on each corner of my eighty-three acres. I fold the map and stuff it in the pocket of my jeans. We're off on a survey mission of our own, to learn the boundaries of our little queendom.

I slip the rope around Gertie's neck and lead her to the door.

The moment I open it, Gertie shoves past me and is out the door as though shot from a cannon. I have a flash of a second to remember I'm holding the other end of her rope before I'm yanked off my feet and down the porch steps, landing with my face in the dirt.

Shock and betrayal hit me at the same time as the pain in my knees. Stiffly, I roll over, only to get a slobbery tongue in my face. Gertie's above me now, licking and pawing.

"Gertie, No! Quit it!" I throw one arm over my face and shove her away with the other.

Instantly, she freezes, then sits down hard. Her expression is so tragic, I can't help laughing. Big as she is, she's only a baby dog. She's got a lot to learn, just like me.

I plant a kiss on the top of her velvety head, rub away the soreness in my knees, and climb stiffly to my feet. Then we're back on schedule.

We head northeast, uphill, until we reach a double strand of barbed wire nailed directly into the trees. We head along this fence line for a while. Now and again, I see white and red tin signs: *Keep Out*. The map in my pocket doesn't say whose land is adjacent to mine. Best guess, this is the boundary of Steen McMasters's property.

Gertie zigzags, yanking me this way and that. The forest floor must read to her nose like a novel.

I inhale, trying to experience these woods as she does, through its scents. The air's full of the smoky perfume of dry leaves, like a premature autumn.

What does she hear? Just a guess, but if I were a dog, I'd be tuned in to the sounds of anything alive. At midday, these woods hum with bird calls and the incessant sizzles, creaks, and jangles of insects. But now I realize, I haven't seen a single racoon, or deer. Aside from the mice in Aunt Colleen's bathrobe pocket, and the snake in the rafters, the mountain seems emptied of animal life. Anything large enough to need a steady supply of water must have moved on once the rain stopped.

The barbed wire takes a sharp right turn to the north. Not far off, I spot a flat greenish-gray rock with a brass disk embedded in its surface. Gertie sniffs it and wanders off to root around a tree stump. I pass my hand over the patina of the metal. Stamped into it are the letters USGS and some numbers, meaningless to me. The first boundary marker.

I slip the map from my pocket, take a guess at the angle from here, and we head downhill, toward what I think is the northern border of our land.

Late in the afternoon, we've found the second marker, and we've just taken a ninety-degree turn to walk the southern border of my land. My face is buried in the map when a sound penetrates through the bottom of my sneakers. A low rumble, half earthquake, half hornet's nest. It's coming from inside of Gertie. She's on full alert at my side, a ridge of fur stands at full mast on the back of her neck. How can my sweet baby dog make such a fearsome sound?

Then it occurs to me to look ahead into the bushes to see what she's growling at. Something is standing perfectly still in the brush just off the path ahead of us. It's jet black. I can't even see its face, yet I know its eyes are fixed on us. I tighten my grip on Gertie's rope.

Presently, the animal walks onto the path. At first, my mind tries to tell me it's a furry deer. Do they have moose in West Virginia? It moves with a rocking, long-legged lope. It pauses and turns its great, round face toward us.

My blood runs cold. It's not a moose.

The bear examines us a long while. It waggles its meaty nose back and forth, puzzling out our scent. Then it trundles slowly toward us, scooping the dust of the trail with its heavy paws.

I'm frozen in my tracks. Gertie stands like a statue, every muscle poised for action.

The bear cocks its head at us. It meets my gaze. A flash of knowing passes between us, the same as when I meet the eye of another human being. Then it sidesteps us, meanders off the trail into the leaves and twigs, and continues on its way.

Little by little, I unfreeze. I turn around to watch the bear departing. Now that my mind has placed it, I realize that this animal is skinny by bear standards. Probably dying. Heading north in search of the one thing it needs more than food.

On the heels of my relief at not becoming bear-chow comes a flood of wonder.

It's the first, and last, large wild animal that I see on my mountain.

We give the bear a long while to remove itself elsewhere. Then we hang a left and continue our survey. As we trek downward, another trail crosses the one we're on. Gertie perks up, snuffles around, and tries to pull me toward it. Something about this trail, she likes. But it winds away from our property, so I gently tug her back onto our path. I can't help wondering where it leads. This mountain has stories to tell, secrets to reveal.

Dusk is rising out of the valley when the woods give way to a ledge of stone overlooking the riverbed. We make our way carefully along the sharp drop-off past the water tower. I stay well back from the edge and hold Gertie's rope close to me, none too eager to see the inside of that tank again.

I stand as close to the edge as I dare—not close at all—and I catch a glimpse of the outskirts of Cooper's Forge: the down-hill road that brought me into town on the first day, the twin gas pumps at Christmas General Store.

An evening sky, soft blue and pearlescent, opens wide before me, naked of clouds, as it has been everywhere in this part of America for more than two years.

I'm looking out on places that could be twenty miles away. A flush of pride overtakes me, that I own a view like this.

"Picnic rock, Gertie. Lunch here tomorrow?" Gertie wags her assent.

I glance down for a good spot to lay a picnic blanket. Inches from the toes of my pink high-tops sits the third brass boundary marker.

One more to go.

We're heading uphill again, trying to spot the final marker before the daylight is spent. All at once, Gertie halts and goes rigid. She's staring in the direction of the cabin. From the back of her head to her shoulder blades, her fur stands up like porcupine bristles. A low rumble begins deep in her throat and erupts from her with a chuffing sound. Her jowls flutter.

I catch a glimmer of flashlight beams through the trees, and I realize just how dark it's already gotten. Our eyes must have been adjusting as the light dimmed.

Someone's at our camp.

My stomach goes icy.

I think, Let's creep back there quietly, hide in the brush, and see what's going on. But Gertie already has a plan of her own. She charges straight for the cabin, towing me behind her at the end of the rope, and announcing our presence with her throaty yodel: "*Yo, Yoooooouuu!*"

Two huge men in light blue work shirts stand outside my cabin. Their bodies are tensed, bracing for whatever's about to charge out of the bushes at them, but when they see it's just me and a half-grown puppy, they relax.

I recognize them: the two meat-stacks that were banished from the main table at Althea's picnic. Bill and Newt. Tweedle Dumb and Tweedle Dipshit. I recognize the logo on their shirts: a turquoise water droplet with the white silhouette of the mountain.

And then Steen himself strolls out my front door.

"Good evening to you, Miss Truax."

"You're in my cabin," I say.

Steen lights up when he sees Gertie. "Look at you, pretty girl!" He leans to pet her. She twists away from his hand.

Bill Pike fixes me with that same empty stare.

"Excuse me. Why are you guys in my house?"

"I heard you had a little trouble the past couple nights. I wanted to make sure you were all right."

"We're good."

"Look, Vicki. Let's put our cards on the table. You know this place isn't for you. You're a career woman; you belong in a city. This was a cute vacation for you. But those assholes who came at you the other night, now they know you're on your own up here. What happens when they show up again, and it's a dozen of them?"

It's not like that same thought hasn't been keeping me awake for days.

"I rescued you once, and I was happy to do it," he says, as though reading my thoughts, "but frankly, I don't have time to be looking after you. So, here's what I propose. I'm going to bail you out."

He steps closer to me than I like. Gertie catches my mood and growls low.

"Your land was appraised when Colleen's estate transferred to you, right? Whatever the appraisal says it's worth, I'll buy it from you for double that amount. Double, Vicki. You won't get a better exit strategy than that."

I hold my breath a long moment. Then I say, "I'll think about it."

Steen flashes a bright grin without a trace of warmth in it. "Yeah. Good. You do that, Vicki." He turns to go. Bill and Newt follow. Bill still hasn't taken his eyes off me.

"Take until tomorrow night to think about it," he says. "After that, the offer expires."

4

When the weather changed every day, I couldn't have cared less about the forecast. Now that we're into our second year without a change, I can't tear myself away. On the edge of Picnic Rock, I can pick up a faint signal. I twist the knob through channel after channel until I find it.

The meteorologist, always apologetic, as though he personally brought on this drought, begins with some version of, "Sorry, folks, I wish I had better news." They tally the number of days since it's rained in our area, steadily approaching six hundred. They repeat the same phrases, "stalled weather system," and "consistent dry pattern."

We were once called the sweet spot: while the rest of the world fried, froze, drowned, or scorched, the mid-Atlantic states got off with a slap on the wrist. Now, we're getting what's due us.

My mountain has a way of screening out the world. Cell phone signals don't reach us. Only one patch of town gets an internet connection, and that's spotty. My laptop used to be a daily feature of my life, but here, it's remained wrapped in T-shirts, tucked in a box. Probably, by now, covered with a sprinkling of mouse poo. Like everything else in this cabin.

Except for the forecast, I don't miss internet news. The news I need now is more immediate than that. I'm learning to read the light that sluices through the trees, the calls of birds, the tiny changes in my woods as summer inches toward fall. Gertie is my reporter. Her superior nose and ears capture the movements of worms under soil, moles burrowing, snakes sunning themselves on rocks. The approach of visitors.

She freezes, head up, nose pointed toward the sound I can't hear yet. Then the *brrraaaaap* of an ATV engine echoes off the parched tree trunks. When the sound is deafening and I'm feeling it through the soles of my boots, Cool Breeze rounds the bend. He pulls up in my yard with his full-arm wave and shit-eating grin.

"Hey there, Miss Vicki! Oh, cool beans, you got yourself a dog."

"Hi, Breeze. Meet Gertie."

Breeze kneels before Gertie, who wags her whole body at him. He takes her jowly face in his hands and then he licks her nose. She licks his in return. Yuck.

"She's from Cleo's bloodline, that's for sure. This pup is the grand-doggie, or maybe even the great-grand-doggie, of your aunt Colleen's dog, Cleo. Cleo was famous around here. They even put her on the ballot for mayor of Cooper's Forge once. You've got to ask Althea to tell you that story some time."

Now Breeze and Gertie are licking all over each other's faces.

"You let her lick your mouth like that?"

"Her tongue's cleaner than mine."

She definitely smells better than he does. He may have a point.

Breeze rises to his feet. "Anyhow, the folks in town wanted me to let you know they routed out a couple of hoodlums from the Springs late last night. Surprised them just as they were trying to sneak back into the old hotel. Had the Harrisonburg sheriff take them away."

"Well, that's a load off my mind."

"Yeah, well, there's bound to be more of them. Good thing you know how to protect yourself. Early said they heard an air-horn go off a night or two ago. Sounded like it might have come from up here?"

Brownie points for the fledgling mountain girl. I earned them; I'll take them. "Yeah. That was me."

Breeze grins wide. "Good for you, Miss Vicki."

He asks me if I need anything. We exchange a few pleasantries, and then, blessed relief, he's on his way back down to town, leaving Gertie and me to enjoy our mountain.

I bring in enough wood to last all night. I prop the coffee pot on the burner, turn it down low, feed Gertie, and settle in to wait out the darkness. Nocturnal is what I must become if I stay here. I'll have to get used to napping during the day.

I fill an enameled tin cup with coffee strong enough to strip paint, settle into Aunt Colleen's rocker, and try to think of ways to keep my mind occupied so I don't fall asleep.

I replay my confrontation with Steen. Take until tomorrow night, he'd said. If he'd come to me even a day before, I might have wavered. If he'd been even slightly less of a jerk about it, I could have considered. But something new is waking up inside of me. My inner lioness. And she does not care for being pushed around. I decide then and there I won't even dignify Steen's offer with a response.

If I leave this place, it will be my own choice, not because some rich boy and his two goons try to push me off it.

A hard yellow moon rises over the ridge across the valley and casts a fractured beam through Aunt Colleen's gray lace curtain. I watch what the moonlight does to my woods. It sparkles through dried leaves and gleams along the undersides of dead branches. I can actually see it rising, changing as it ascends, from pale gold to milk-white, to a cold and bloodless non-color that sets every leaf in silhouette and throws sharp-edged shadows all across the forest floor.

Anyone who dares set foot in my yard tonight, I'll see them before they take two steps.

Now the moon is high above us, unearthly and small. Nothing outside my window looks real. I'm not asleep, but it's as if my mind has thinned.

I know without seeing that an owl holds vigil in the pine tree on the far side of the clearing, waiting for a mouse to make the fatal error of showing itself. I'm aware of moths fanning their wings in the bloodless light, of termites grinding away at rotted wood, of snakes dreaming in their burrows.

The first thing I notice is that the hair on the back of my neck is standing straight out from my skin. Then I become aware that the cicadas have fallen silent. Gertie, who was snoring with her head on my feet, is now standing at full attention with her hackles up. A deep growl vibrates in her throat.

I scan the edge of the yard. I can't see who's there; he must be standing just inside the shadows. But his presence is written on every cell in my body. Now I test the limits of my new non-sight: I try to work out where, precisely, this person is standing.

Yes. He's there, just beside the wood pile. I reach behind me in the dark, fumbling for the fire poker.

All at once, Gertie blasts past me, knocking me aside and throwing the door wide. She launches straight for the spot near the woodpile. A figure breaks cover and hurtles away.

"Gertie, no! Get back here!"

Gertie chases the intruder down the mountain. Twigs snap, underbrush crashes. Gertie tells the world she's in full pursuit: "*Yooooouuu! Yooooouuu!*" Her yodeling cry grows fainter as she follows her quarry downhill. Then, the mountain falls silent.

I'm out the door after her before I have time to think about what I'm doing, pounding downhill along a rocky, root-tangled trail lit only by moonlight. I only half-know the first part of this trail. I'm already careening down a part of the mountain I've never been on before.

The mountainside falls away steeper and now I'm doing everything I can just to remain on my feet. I can't even hear Gertie. The name of this game is, get onto some level ground, girl, before you snap an ankle.

I'm hurtling headlong into thick, prickly brambles, moving far too fast to control my direction. Gravity has me completely. Thorns scrape my hands and branches whip my face, but at least they slow my descent.

All at once, the bushes spit me out and my feet hit hard on level ground. I'm out in the open, on a gravel road. The moonlight is so bright, I stand blinking, waiting for my eyes to adjust. The road ahead of me is flanked with two concrete columns topped with statues of what might have once been swans. One is missing both wings; the other is minus its head. A heavy black chain sags between the two columns.

Beyond the columns, I make out the shapes of buildings: enormous, lightless, and silent. The still air is thick with the scent of rotted wood. In an instant, I know where I am. Exactly where I shouldn't be.

Once my legs stop shaking, I step over the black chain and move silently in among the buildings. A sharp pain knifes me from inside my chest and I remember to breathe.

What might have been a guard house, or a porter's cottage, stands stripped of its door, with its two windows smashed. It looks like a surprised jack-o'-lantern, mouth open in a perma-nent scream. The entry to Kelso Springs is dotted with white concrete pillars and the remains of statues.

Now I come to the first of the guest houses. I recognize them from Althea's postcard. The paint on these stately build-ings dangles in long ribbons from their porch ceilings. Some of their balconies have collapsed into piles of giant matchsticks. Years' worth of fallen leaves are heaped on their stairs and porches like brittle snowdrifts. Not a single window remains unbroken. The bathing pools I remember from the postcard are full of branches, old tires, and debris. In one, the snow-white head of a Grecian statue lies at an angle, half buried in rotted rags. I ache for the lost dignity of the place.

A tingle washes through me. I've seen no lights, heard no movement. And yet, my new-found mountain sense is telling me someone is watching me out of those ruined windows. I'm already too far in to turn back. I keep on, heading toward the great hotel, for lack of any better destination.

The deeper into Kelso Springs I go, the more dreamlike everything becomes. Without sound, without wind, and in the unnatural light of that high, distant moon, I can't escape the sensation that I'm swimming through the silver-lit air. Each step forward could be taking hours to complete, or it all could have happened years ago.

I take in the ruined balconies; my memory transposes images of the happy young people who once adorned them. They probably danced up there. A night like this would have been full of lantern-light and roses, of laughter and stolen smooches and candlelight gleaming on water.

I'm so deep into this dream, I'm nearly seeing them. A movement on the road ahead catches my eye. I'm dreaming of a man walking toward me. He's soundless, like the bathers I'm imagining on the balconies. Too tall for his slender frame, and ghostly pale. He carries a plastic jerry can in either hand.

I stand completely still until he's within a few feet of me. His glasses flash in the moonlight, so I can't see the expression in his eyes. A silver beard covers most of the lower half of his face. I can't read the expression there, but I can guess he isn't smiling.

He stares at me for a long moment, then whispers huskily, "What in hell do you think you're doing?"

"I'm going to get my dog."

"If they took her, your dog's dead already."

A spike of anger hits me between the eyes. Ghostly as he looks, I'll bet he's real enough to feel a swift kick.

"You don't know that."

"They know who you are. They'd kill her just to send you a message." The pale man turns his head to gesture at the ghostly buildings. His white ponytail whips across his shoulder.

At last, I'm convinced I'm not dreaming. "Alaric?"

He rolls his eyes.

I start to pass around him.

"They'll shoot you!" The urgency in his husky voice stops me in my tracks.

I turn back. "Well, what about you? Why didn't they shoot you if they're so trigger-happy?"

In response, he lifts the jerry cans and raises his eyebrows.

"So, if they love their water-guy so much, why don't you go tell them to give her back to me?"

"I'll get you another damn dog. Don't be a fool."

My courage is slipping away fast. I step around him and march toward the main hotel.

Now I'm making my way up the ruined walkway and onto the porch of the grand building. The rotted wood groans beneath my feet. I feel with my toes to make sure the floor will hold me before I put my full weight down. The boards flex beneath my feet, but so far, they're solid.

The carved front doors have their window glass smashed out. I push on them and they swing inward stiffly. A grand foyer opens before me. I catch a scent of candle wax. I stand in the center of the room. I hum quietly to myself to get my voice working, to make sure it's not going to quaver, then I call out, "I'm just here for my dog."

This place is full of echoes: wood creaking, walls sighing, what could be footsteps somewhere above me, but might simply be the echoes of my own footfalls. Only one way to know.

At the far end of the foyer, two staircases lead upward to the second floor. Both have all their stairs. Either one might hold me. I choose the one to the left, climb it, and find myself staring into a long dark corridor flanked with doors on either side. A picture window at the far end of the hallway lets in a smudge of moonlight. So many doors, so many rooms to check. And this is only the first floor.

I'm wrapping my fingers around the first doorknob when one of the doors at the far end of the corridor creaks open. A triangle of orange light spills out onto the floor. I hear whispers, maybe. Then a small figure steps into the corridor.

This person's back is to the moonlit window; I can see nothing but a black silhouette, moving slowly, with great difficulty, carrying a large, heavy object.

My heart knocks hard against my ribcage. I stand and wait for the person to approach. All at once, a rhythmic thudding echoes in the hallway. There's something immediately comforting about this sound: the thwack of a furry tail against fabric.

Now the stranger emerges from the darkness of the corridor into the half-light at the top of the stairs: a girl, smudged and tangle-haired, no more than twelve. My throat tightens. She carries Gertie, nearly the same weight as her. And, except for the tail, thumping the girl's shoulder even harder the closer she gets to me, Gertie is keeping obediently still. Her four legs dangle down comically from the girl's arms. The girl passes beneath a stray beam of light that reveals her copper-colored hair and two solemn blue eyes. She sets Gertie down when she's still a car's length away from me. Gertie rushes at me, throws two paws up on my chest, and bounces on her hind legs, trying to reach my face with her tongue. The girl turns and runs. The door at the end of the corridor slams shut.

I've used up every last scrap of my courage. Gertie and I sprint down the stairs, across the foyer, down the porch steps, and down the gravel road. I rely on Gertie's nose to find the entry to the path that takes us back up the mountain.

Time has started running again because the hike back up the mountain takes forever. I have time to calm down. To come to my senses. To hug my dog and thank God for letting me get her back. And then, when we're nearly back to the cabin, to think, that little girl was pretty damn young for a moonshiner.

I let us into the cabin and bolt the door behind us. I lean against the rough wood for a moment, knee-bending relief flooding through me at having a door to close between me and rest of the world.

As I kick off my boots and curl up under the covers with Gertie, one last thought crosses my mind before sleep drags me under: I met Alaric tonight. And he's got some 'splainin' to do.

5

Over breakfast, it occurs to me I have a good idea where to find him.

Gertie and I set out to retrace our steps from the day we walked the boundaries of our land. We follow the barbed wire to where the trail turns left. We meander downhill until Gertie sniffs out the cross-trail and wags her excitement.

This time, we do it her way. We turn onto the trail and follow it, through tall blond grass and brambles, past a jutting boulder of gray-green rock, and down toward the dry riverbed.

A voice comes from the rocky outcrop behind us: "You're wasting your time."

I turn a fast one-eighty. Alaric is perched on top of the rock. "You'll only find me if I want to be found."

We must have walked right past him. He's good if he can evade Gertie's nose and ears. When she sees it's him, she goes straight into her full-body wag.

"So, today you must have wanted us to find you," I say.

He doesn't smile. I wait for him to say something more. I recall Susan and Althea telling me how tough he is to talk to. So, I cut to the chase.

"Your pals at the Springs gave me back my dog. And they didn't shoot me."

"So I see."

A spike of anger rises in my throat. "No thanks to you. They're rooting around my land every night and they're trying to frighten me off it. You said yourself they'd kill me and then you just left me there. In fact, you're helping them."

"If I help them, does that hurt you?"

"You're giving them water."

"You think I shouldn't?"

"Well, if they're criminals."

"Are they not also human beings?"

He has me there. Even if I wouldn't have given water to a bunch of thugs, the little girl changes everything. My mama always taught me to be my best self. Best Vicki would have made sure a child had food and water, no matter whose child she was.

"You know there's a child there?"

"That's new. They're starting to bring their families."

"And you're okay with that?"

"Christ, woman, do you not read the news?"

Not lately, no. But I already know things are breaking down in the world outside Cooper's Forge. The green of our mountain must stand out like a beacon in a sea of brown. Of course, people will go where they think there's water.

Alaric rises from his perch and hops like a mountain goat down the rocks to land beside us on the trail. In the sun, he's just as ghostly pale as he was by moonlight. He's what Thora would call freakishly tall. He's not young, but I can't even pin his age to a decade. He could be a hard-living fifty or a well-preserved seventy.

"I know what's happening out there," I tell him. "Before I came here, I was living it. In my city, people were dying every day. Anybody who could get out, well—"

"I'm going to guess something about you; you tell me if I'm right. Back in that city you came from, you made sure people had water, even if they couldn't get it for themselves. Yes or no?"

A hot tide of shame washes over me. The image of Mr. Rosen swims before my eyes. Lying half out of his wheelchair, gasping out his last parched breath.

"I wasn't very good at it."

"You couldn't have saved them all."

Alaric bends down and touches his forehead to Gertie's. She quiets her wriggling and gazes into his eyes. Then he straightens up and looks me in the eye.

"What I'm about to show you, you're not to discuss with

anyone else. Then after that, if it pleases you, we'll have a cup of tea, and you can meet Gertie's family."

It hardly sounds like a request. If he were anyone else, I'd respond with a hell, no. But he's appealing to my curiosity.

"Okay. Sure. Let's go."

We're a long time hiking his side of the mountain. The river valley that cradles Cooper's Forge goes on for much longer than I'd thought. A hawk rides the thermals across the hot, quiet air. Cicadas wind up for their evening concert. It's rockier here, with fewer large trees. Here, as on my side of the mountain, the biggest trees still cling to life, their roots deep enough to tap the mountain's reserves.

Alaric points to a spot on the trail ahead of us where a length of twine runs across at ankle-height. Hanging from it are bits of glass and scraps of tin. He steps over the contraption and motions for me to do the same. Gertie, not keen to snag her floppy ears on anything, skirts around it. A few yards later, he steps over another line, similarly bejeweled with junk.

The third time we come to one of these, I'm on the verge of asking what they're for. Then I figure it out. It's to announce the arrival of intruders. Appalachian doorbell.

The trail turns stony and narrow. Black rocks rise up to flank us. I'm picking my way carefully, indulging visions of twisted ankles, but Alaric trundles along, dodging each rock, as if he makes this trek every day. Which, I realize, he probably does.

The trail turns abruptly downhill, widens, and joins a set of dusty tire tracks. At a thick clump of brambles, Alaric pauses. He throws his arms around the clump, lifts the entire mass, and says, "Well, go on."

Where the brush had been sitting, a tiny track continues up the mountain. Gertie and I go ahead while he sets the armload down behind us.

The trail disappears into a crevice of black rock. A slight puff of air seeps from the dark interior. It's cool on my cheek, and wet.

Alaric shifts past me and draws a flashlight from the pocket of his shorts. By its tiny beam, the three of us edge into the crevice. Its walls are smooth, damp, and give off a scent of minerals. The rock gleams in the flashlight beam, as though polished. I run the flat of my palm over it. It has a patina, like fine mahogany. Many hands have touched the place I'm touching now.

My senses are still reveling in the feel of the stone when a sound begins to reach them: the silvery music of trickling water. Alaric shines his light on the seam in the rock where the liquid emerges. It cascades down the rock face to a shallow basin.

"Drink," Alaric commands.

I scoop a double handful. Shockingly cold. It goes down smooth. Miles better than when it's been sitting in jerry cans on my porch for a few hours, growing tepid in the sun.

The water flows steadily into the stone basin but doesn't overflow. There must be a pipe that leads out somewhere.

"I don't understand. People are dying. Why would you keep this a secret?"

Alaric rolls up the sleeve of his shirt and plunges his hand into the basin. He comes up with a brass-lidded Mason jar half-full of a thick, ivory-colored liquid, wipes it on his shirt, and hands it to me.

"The townsfolk introduce you to their famous biscuits?"

"Yeah, I think I had some at a picnic a few days ago. They're amazing."

"The secret is right there in your hands. That's one-hundred-year-old sourdough starter."

Alaric leads the way back down the path, holds the brush aside for me, and then takes us the rest of the way down the slope. The trail empties out on a stretch of red and brown gravel. Along the forest edge, a few of the shrubs are clinging to life. Alaric points to one.

"Shape of the leaves. Teardrop. Mitten. Chicken foot. Three kinds of leaves on one bush. Dig right there at the base."

"With what?"

"You've got hands."

The soil comes away lightly under my fingers, although my manicurist would be none too pleased with what I've just done to myself. I dig until a long, feathery root, like a spindly gray carrot, pokes from the soil.

"Twist that off."

I do, although not gracefully. The broken root gives off a surprisingly familiar aroma. Sweet, rich, herbal. A scent from childhood.

"Now you know how to dig sassafras."

We follow the gravelly riverbank a while. In the distance comes a full-throated call, "*Yo! Yooooouuu!*" It's taken up by many more canine voices. Gertie tips back her head and yodels in answer.

Further on, the riverbed opens onto a meadow of tall dry grass that stretches to the foot of the rock cliffs. We swish through the grass until we come to a twig fence. Inside it, the shorn grass gleams yellow-green, three floppy-eared brown and white goats graze, black-and-gray striped chickens waddle, and a cabin not so different from Aunt Colleen's stands with its back to the mountain.

Four enormous hounds race to meet us and follow us along the inside of the fence. They're red-brown and black, wrinkled and rumpled as though the skins they're in are three sizes too large for them. Their velvet ears hang almost to the ground.

Three of them galumph about on oversized paws, just like Gertie.

"That's Diana. This one's Madea. Here's Hercules."

The fourth dog is nearly twice the size of the others. From the shoulders back, she could be a slender lioness.

"And this one's Freya. Gertie's mama."

I snuggle and smooch each dog in turn. The goats race over for their share of cuddles.

"Do you actually milk these goats?" As the words leave my lips, I nearly cringe at what a city girl I sound like.

"It takes water to make milk. Right now, I can only give them enough to live on."

A cream-colored goat gazes up at me with her bizarre, bar-shaped pupils.

"So then, what are they for?"

Alaric tosses me a withering gaze. "What are *you* for?"

He opens a gate I hadn't seen, and motions for me to enter.

While Gertie romps with her family, we make up a panful of sourdough biscuits, bake them on Alaric's coil, and wash them down with cups of hot sassafras tea.

Alaric doesn't ask me anything; he just waits for me to speak. Once I start telling him about myself, my story just keeps flowing. By nightfall, he knows more than many people who have known me for years, about my life on Delaney Street, my work as an editor, my divorce, what it was like watching Baltimore dry up and die around me. He keeps listening, so I keep talking.

The moon is a silver coin at the top of the sky and the cicadas are in full voice before he finally turns the conversation back to the water. I get a sense that he may know more about this place even than Althea. So, I ask him.

"That hotel kept going for many years. Before Kelso Springs were coal miners, and before them, barrel makers. They all tapped the mountain and hit pockets of water. None of them knew about that spring. But the people before them knew it, a long time ago. Long before European people came to this mountain, that spring had a name."

I wait. But Alaric seems to be done speaking.

"And the name was?"

"You wouldn't understand."

"Try me."

"I'd have to explain it. Your generation doesn't have the patience."

"Maybe I'm not like the rest of my generation."

He lets out a long sigh, as though he's already regretting this turn of conversation. Then, as if settling in to tell a long story, he says, "The way our kind behaves toward water has changed. So, water has changed the way it behaves toward us."

I shift in my seat uncomfortably. Alaric looks up at me

sharply. "You disagree?"

"No, it's just this conversation might be getting a little too supernatural for my taste."

He rises. "You're not ready to hear this."

I stay in my seat. "Yes, I am."

He sighs. Tugs at his beard. Studies me for a long moment. Then he sits back in his chair and says, "Most people need to know more than their eyes and ears can give them. You call it supernatural. They might call it an explanation for the unexplainable. Do you think that makes you superior to them?"

"No, it's just…"

The thing about Alaric, he doesn't talk over me. I expect him to cut me off, but he's waiting, eyebrows raised, for me to finish my sentence. I hadn't even planned on finishing it. I have time to think through my answer. It's a luxury most people have never given me.

"It's just, I took sociology in college. The myth of the eco-savage. The un-historied people living in paradise until the white man came along. It's a modern invention."

"Well, then. That's that." He sips his tea.

"But…I am open to learning something else."

There's nothing more I can do but sit quietly and see if he'll begin again. For a long while, he's silent. He might be testing me, to see if I'm serious enough to wait for it.

He reaches toward the stack of firewood by his hearth and holds up a splintery chunk of log. "What's this?"

"A piece of wood?"

He holds up his half-eaten biscuit. "And this?"

"A chunk of biscuit."

He takes a tin mug from the wall, fills it from the water flask, and raises it. "What about this?"

"A cup of water."

"And if I do this," he pours from the cup into his open palm, "what do I have in my hand?"

"A handful of water?"

"That's how our people think. We put everything in com-

partments. To the people who lived here before, this idea of
'a piece of water' would have made no sense. To them, there
was only 'the waters.' A river, a lake, an ocean, a well. All one,
indivisible. When they went to bathe, when they went to drink,
they called it, 'going to the waters.'"

Alaric tips the palm of his hand, and the water spatters
onto the dusty floorboards of his cabin. As I watch the wood
turn dark and the water seep between the cracks, he continues,
"They told each other stories about the calamities that would
happen if they pissed in the waters, or dirtied the waters with
the blood of animals, or if they took the waters for granted."

He hands me the cup. "To them, they were the domain of
tortured and terrifying creatures, lying in wait to seek vengeance
on someone who disrespected the waters. Can you not see how
differently you would live in the world, if that were how you
thought?"

"Oh," I say quietly, peering into the cup. I imagine it as a
dark well, without a bottom. Shapeless creatures slithering in
its depths.

"The people who lived on this mountain a long time ago,
they thought of a river as though it were a person. A river to
them was a long, long man, with his head in the mountains and
his feet in the sea."

I picture a tall, silver-gray man, wavy and bendy. A river delta
would be his arms and legs, fingers, and toes. If his head is in
the mountains, then water from a mountain well would be like
thoughts, springing into his mind.

"What cooled the coopers' saws and miners' drills and filled
Kelso Springs. What the people of this town live on. What
the moonshiners come for. What you've been drinking. What
you've given your dog to drink. The water for your tea. It's all
from *tsiskoli ada asgaya*. The Head of the Long Man."

"That was its name?"

Alaric nods.

I ask him to repeat the name. I try saying it, tasting the foreign words on my tongue.

We finish our tea in silence. We step out into the dark and I give each of the dogs a kiss. Alaric walks Gertie and me back to the place where his path joins up with my land.

As he turns to go, I call after him, "I haven't thanked you for Gertie. And all the water and food."

"You're not terrible to talk with. You can come back if you want. Just don't wear out your welcome."

∾

I wake in late morning with a fully formed conviction. I see my mistake: waiting for them to come onto my land, intimidate me, wreck my food, steal my dog. That ends today.

I eat a can of peaches; Gertie wolfs down a bowlful of kibble. We head out of the cabin as soon as we're done. I spot two new jerry cans of water resting on my porch: Alaric strikes again.

We walk the forest track down the east side of the mountain and into town. I manage to avoid the townsfolk. I find my nasty green Chevy still in its spot behind Christmas General Store. After a few cranks of the ignition, it starts up for me. Gertie hangs her head out of the passenger side window and we drive through tiny, parched towns until we find a hardware store that's still open: a little white clapboard shop on the corner with an oval sign, Campbell's Hardware.

Ten minutes later, we're on our way back to Cooper's Forge with a hundred yards of twine, two dozen short pieces of metal pipe, and a paper sack full of bolts. We park the Chevy and manage to get back up the mountain without having to talk to anybody. We're not wasting time today.

I work fast. I tie a good six inches of twine to each of the bolts and hang them inside the pipes. Then with pipes and bolts slung clanking over my shoulder, I set off into the woods.

I no longer keep Gertie on a rope. She hugs my side most of the time, and when she does wander off, chasing some enticing new smell, she comes right back again in a moment. She never lets me out of her sight.

I start nearest the cabin. I tie a strand of twine from one sapling to another, a few yards away, right below knee height. Then I hang a pipe and bolt on the line. I lean on the strand to test it. The bolt clatters musically against the inside of the pipe.

I move to another clump of saplings some distance apart and rig up another strand of twine with its noisemaker. And then another. I work my way down the mountain in a widening zigzag. By late afternoon, I'm out of twine, and Gertie and I have rigged up a low-tech intruder alert system on our property: our very own Appalachian doorbell.

We're on our way back to the cabin when Gertie freezes and lets out a low growl. Through the trees, I see a black ATV parked in our yard. Sweet Jesus, can people not leave us in peace for one day?

A man in a navy-blue shirt and mirrored sunglasses waits on the front porch as we walk up.

"Victoria Louise Truax?"

"Yes?"

He holds out a dark yellow envelope. Reflexively, I take it. "You've been served, ma'am." He strides past me, climbs aboard his ATV, and rides away.

It's only a few printed pages, but an hour later, I'm still trying to read it through the flashes of red that swim before my eyes.

Parsing the legalese, I work out three facts: one, during Aunt Colleen's final days on Earth, she was too busy dying to pay her property taxes, resulting in the state putting a lien on the land.

Two, in the State of West Virginia, if someone else pays off a tax lien on a piece of property, and the landowner doesn't repay that person in a period of time that has now apparently lapsed, that person can apply for a hearing to claim ownership of the land.

According to these papers, someone has done precisely that, and the case will be heard in court two months from today.

And three, that person is Steen McMasters.

೨

Althea's kitchen is painted a shade of yellow that puts me in mind of banana pudding. Or pancake batter. I'm sitting at her little round melamine table, gulping back tears, while she pours me a mug of what I think is sweet tea. When she places it before me, my nose tingles from the fumes. Smoky, peaty, straight-up Kentucky-style bourbon.

I picked the right place for a melt-down.

Althea pours herself a mugful and sits down across from me. Her two Scotty dogs have tackled Gertie and she's paws-up in surrender on the linoleum floor, while they romp across her belly.

"You got the advantage."

"I do?"

Althea doesn't sit in her chair; she spreads into it. "He underestimates you." She taps a gnarled finger against the court papers on the table between us. "The kind of enemy who makes that mistake, he's the easiest to beat."

I hold a sip of the bourbon in my mouth, loll it around with my tongue. Its honey-sweetness gives way to a warmth that turns to a burn I have to swallow. It stings all the way down my throat. The smokiness lingers long after the liquid's gone.

Somewhere in my gullet, a sob is trying to escape. I distract myself by letting my eyes linger on Althea's living room décor. Needlepoint scenes of English countryside. Lots of plaques. A hammer-like object in a glass case the Baltimorean in me takes to be a crab mallet.

"You want to cry, gal, you just go on and cry." She offers me a cigarette and I shake my head.

"Althea, I haven't got the slightest idea what to do."

"Now, that ain't so."

One of the Scotties quits torturing Gertie and lollops up beside Althea. He rolls over and exposes his tubby gray belly, which she strokes with the toe of her slipper. "You just ain't worked out what it is you want. You figure that out, you'll know what to do."

I stare into my bourbon. Something deep inside me relaxes. There's a reason Aunt Colleen called this woman a friend. When she's right, she's right.

"Althea, did you ever meet my dad?" The words slip out of my mouth without a forethought. Her bourbon's worse for my judgment than Steen's bathtub gin.

To say Althea's face goes steely wouldn't mean much because that's her normal expression. But I think I detect a shadow descending in her eyes. My question's not pleasant to her.

After a beat, she says, "Colleen had a sister. Sister had a child. Child grew up, had a child of his own, abandoned his family. That ain't the Cooper's Forge way. And that's all you need to know."

I will myself to go to sleep early that night, but every time I close my eyes, they fly right back open again. The bourbon headache I acquired at Althea's isn't helping, either. Liquor consumption in a time of drought: not a plan.

I roll onto my side. Then onto my belly. Whichever way I turn, the ropes under Aunt Colleen's mattress dig into some part of me.

Althea's words of advice weave in and out of the bourbon fog. Do I know what I want? Yes. I want to be home.

Is this home?

It's the closest I've known to belonging. Unlikely as it is that a born-and-bred city girl would fit into a tiny Appalachian town, these people have made room for me; they count me as one of their own. As far as they're concerned, I belong.

When Mama was alive, I never questioned my place in this world: she was always the center of my universe. Without her, I became a rogue planet, spinning out into empty space. Now, I find myself settling into orbit among the kin of the stranger who donated half my genes and nothing more. Someone I never knew.

When the darkness turns bloodless and cold enough to be four o'clock in the morning, I rise, grab my flashlight, and slip out of the cabin. Gertie jumps to her feet and falls in behind me.

As we cross the boundary between my land and Alaric's, we can see headlights piercing the half-dry foliage. The flatbed Ford with the plastic stock tank I had seen in town idles in front of the entrance to Alaric's spring. I catch a gleam of his white hair; he's behind the truck, rolling up a ribbed green hose. The brimming-full tank casts watery shadows in my flashlight beam.

When he sees my light, he turns toward me. He squints in my direction. Then he points to a row of jerry cans. "You can fill those up."

Gertie wags her way over to him and leans against his legs. He bends, cups her jowls in his hands, and gazes into her eyes. He doesn't lick her face like Breeze does, or cuddle her like I do, but something good passes between them.

I heft two of the cans, push through the brush, and dunk them in the cistern. The water seems a lot further down than when I'd first put my lips to it, but then, Alaric did just fill a giant tank from it. We tag team, back and forth until the cans are filled.

Alaric directs me to heft ten of them onto the rear deck of the truck. He tightens them down with rope. He points to Gertie. "Put her in the cabin with my pups." Then he climbs into the cab.

After I stow Gertie and climb in on the passenger side, we rattle our way down a pelvis-numbing dirt track, then join a gravel road. At the end this road, he turns onto the one-lane highway heading toward Cooper's Forge.

He pulls up alongside the twin statues that mark the entrance to the Springs. Together, we untie four of the jerry cans and hoist them down from the truck. I pick up two and make ready for the hike in.

"You stay with the truck," Alaric says.

"But they know me now. And I'm with you."

Alaric turns to face me. He can say more with no words at all than most people say with a mouthful of them. I set down the cans.

"Just give them to her," Alaric gestures to a clump of bush-es. All at once, I see a human form waiting silently just outside the lights. As I hand over the cans, I catch a glimpse of a dirty yellow bandana around her head. Then he and the woman turn and head for Kelso Springs.

I wait in the cab for Alaric. My feet go numb. I need to pee. I fiddle with the radio. It creeps me out: the white noise and the ghosts of stations I can't quite tune in by the weak dashboard light. All the while, somewhere down that gravel road, within the moldering ruins of elegant buildings, a group of murderous people wait, unseen and silent, for their water.

A sliver of turquoise light has already begun to bloom on the east ridge when Alaric returns.

On the road into town, I say, "Why didn't you let me come?"

"Desperate people aren't your friends."

"So, you bring them water, but you won't let them know where your spring is."

Alaric pulls a paper pouch down from the sun visor, takes out a squarish lump, and tucks it into his cheek. He fishes in the pouch for another and holds it out to me. I hate tobacco, but one glance at his face and I gauge that I've pissed him off enough for one morning. I take it and copy his movement.

It's not tobacco. The wrap of leaves taste all at once peachy, peppery, and like fresh-cut grass. My mouth fills with sweet liquid.

He moves his leaf-quid around in his mouth and says slowly, "In Honduras, they give fruit to the sea."

I'm beginning to think Alaric is the king of non sequiturs. I wait for him to go on.

"They take the best of their harvest. Build little straw boats. Fill them with fruit and float them out to sea. It's an offering. To make sure the sea keeps giving them what they need."

Alaric gives more thinking-room in a conversation than anyone else I've known. He seems to expect me to draw some kind of conclusion from what he's said. All at once, I'm embarrassed. I don't want him to think I'm dense.

Finally, curiosity gets the better of me. "I don't get it. I mean, I know it's a metaphor. So, in this case, you're the sea. You give these people the water they need. What 'fruit'—what offering—are they giving you?"

"They let me stay alive."

"You know, I'm not convinced they're all that dangerous. I think maybe you just do it because you're nice."

"Nice!" he roars.

By the sickly morning light, I see. Alaric is smiling.

We deliver two jerry cans each to Lila's and Althea's front porches. In front of the church, we unhook the trailer and leave the tank in its place for the day.

Once back at Alaric's compound, I reunite with Gertie. Alaric straps the remaining jerry cans to his dirt bike. These are for Early Slade, on the other side of the valley.

Alaric points to the last two jerry cans. "Those are yours. Take those with you and save me the trip."

Just as I'm settling in to sleep off the morning's work, Cool Breeze rolls up. He's come to fetch me to gather black walnuts. Instead of a long snooze and quiet day alongside my dog, I'm cracking my pelvis, jouncing against the rear seat of Breeze's ATV as we *braaappp* down the mountain, Gertie lolloping along behind.

The grove of wild walnut trees stands at the edge of a cow pasture minus its cows, close to the crevice of cracked mud that, Susan tells me, was once a creek.

She whaps my arm with a pair of latex gloves. "Here, darlin'. Them's so you don't stain your hands."

She introduces me to Happ, the owner of this land. He takes my hand as reverently as if it were a Fabergé egg. "Good to meet ya, ma'am."

I can't suppress a giggle.

"I'm not that old, Happ. No need to ma'am me."

Happ blushes and grins, charming me silly.

The townsfolk are tackling the task at hand with an earnestness that no mere nuts should be worthy of. They complain bitterly at how few there are, but within five minutes, I'm convinced there's way too many of the damn things. The fingers of my gloves are stained a deep mahogany; so is one thumb where the latex ripped. The fuzzy, rock-hard green fruits that protect the walnuts ping like a hammer-strike as we toss them into Breeze's aluminum trailer. They leave dents if we toss them in too hard.

When the trailer is full of the nasty-smelling things, I think the work is done. But the townsfolk mount their quads and dirt bikes and gun their engines.

"Where are we taking this shit?" I ask as I climb onto the seat behind Breeze.

He grins. "Your place!"

And with a snarl of little engines, we're off, before I can get another word in.

It turns out, the flat patch of rocks by Aunt Colleen's cabin, where I ate breakfast on my first morning here, is the best walnut-cracking spot for miles around. I guess from the ease with which they make themselves at home, shelling walnuts at Aunt Colleen's is an annual Cooper's Forge ritual.

The folks scatter a few shovels-full of walnuts over the face of a rock, lay a sheet of plywood over them, then beat the bejesus out of the wood with sledgehammers. When one crew of nut-beaters tires, another set jumps up and takes over.

Chunks of walnut shell in our hair, down our shirt collars, up our noses. Splashes of dark brown walnut juice on our jeans. The pounding of steel mallet-heads on wood. The ache in my arms from swinging my hammer. I was never a big fan of walnuts. After today, I don't know if I'll ever stand the sight of them again. But it's worth it for the chance to watch my neighbors working together, and to work alongside them, even at something as pointless as burning a thousand calories to get at fifty calories-worth of musty nuts.

Gertie keeps the four-legged guests entertained with a game of steal-the-stick. Once they've worn themselves out and wagged themselves silly, they flop down on the leaves to pant, flakes of bark in their jowls. Tom and Susan's young shepherd, Henry, lurks perpetually in Gertie's shadow. Tank and Dozer, Happ's barrel-chested pitbulls, lie wriggling on their backs, kicking their feet in the air. Mack and Tippy's red and white pointer, Maggie, the elder states-dog of the group, sits apart from the rowdier bunch. The Dogs of Cooper's Forge.

Cooper's Forge folks go nowhere without their dogs. To a Baltimorean, a dog is a silky pooch riding in a faux alligator handbag, a living accessory. Here, they're co-workers, family.

When the work seems to be winding down, I yell out the cabin door, "Would you guys like me to put on some coffee?" Nods all around.

Minutes later, we've pulled up some logs, chairs, and rocks. We're sipping from Aunt Colleen's enameled tinware. Nobody mentions my legal entanglement with Mister Water Baron, the mood is too light and the day's work too heavy, but something in my neighbor's eyes tells me they know. Cooper's Forge keeps no secrets.

"I expect we'd better think about giving up coffee," Tom muses into his cup. "The caffeine makes us lose body water."

"Coffee just makes me piss," Rennie contributes.

"TMI, Rennie. TMI."

"I miss swimming," Rennie says. "Think we'll ever go swimming again?"

Breeze sits up in his chair. His eyes gleam. "Well, heck. Want to go swimming right now, just not in water?"

"In what, then? Althea's rhubarb jam?"

Breeze is all a-twinkle. He's up and patting Rennie out of his chair. "Folks, I think we just invented ourselves a new sport."

"What're you two up to now?"

Already halfway down the trail, Breeze calls over his shoulder, "You'll see!"

"Oh lordy, what are them two fools going to do to themselves this time?"

A couple hours later, Breeze calls us up to the hill behind my cabin. They've attached a cable to two trees at a barely perceptible downward angle. They've leaned an aluminum painter's ladder against the higher tree and hammered in a wooden packing pallet at the intersection of two thick branches. Rennie stands on the pallet in blue and yellow bathing trunks and swim fins, a snorkel mask perched on his forehead. He's buckling on a climbing harness and clipping it to a heart-shaped metal device on the cable.

As we gather below, Breeze climbs the ladder to stand on the pallet beside Rennie. He checks the harness and the clip. Then he bellows in a ringmaster's voice, "Ladies and gentlemen, I give to you the new sporting sensation that'll put old Cooper's Forge on the map: air swimming!"

Rennie lowers his mask onto his face, puts his two palms together, and dives off the platform. For a moment, Rennie is suspended in midair. He does a breaststroke, kicking his legs like a frog, and slowly begins the descent down the cable. His strokes become more vigorous and he picks up steam, zipping down the cable toward the other tree. The folks hoot and clap and cheer him on. When he lands gracefully on a second packing pallet in the downhill tree, the group erupts in cheers.

All at once, there's a line of people at the base of the higher tree, waiting their turn to swim.

"Come on, Vicki Truax. Don't you want to go swimming?"

"I'll pass. I'm just going to watch you guys make fools of yourselves."

They knock together a second zip line, parallel to the first, and then it becomes a race. It ends with a bunch of grown men standing around in their swim trunks, wearing inflatable ducky rings, floaty Zebras, pink swim goggles and fins, doing their best rendition of "Baby Jaws."

If my phone hadn't run out of battery, I'd be taking pictures.

Then, if I ever needed to blackmail any of these boys, I'd be all set.

It doesn't stop there. Against the backdrop of their laughter and carrying-on, I doze off in the late afternoon sunshine, and when I come to, there's Rennie and Breeze, *in kayaks*, on the two top platforms of the zip line. Breeze sits in a lime-green boat, Rennie in one the color of a pumpkin.

"Look here, Vicki Truax!" Breeze yells down to me. "Air kayaking!"

It would be one thing if they'd zipped their harnesses to the cables and simply held themselves in the kayaks with their legs. But these fools have simply draped climbing harnesses around the front and back of the boats.

"Not a plan, guys, not a plan!"

But they're already launching, paddling the air, and whooping. Rennie's in the lead. Breeze paddles frantically to keep up. Rennie's got some real speed now. Then the front of his kayak slips out of the harness. He's free-falling, still paddling. His kayak hits the ridge at the end of my yard with a thump and keeps going. Rennie and his kayak are airborne when we lose sight of him. He's still crashing along through the brush, whooping his way down the mountain.

My heart jolts. I'm running for him when I hear branches crack. I freeze, dreading what must have just happened.

A moment later, he yodels again. "Woo-hoo-hoooo! Beat that one, bro!"

I race to the crest of the slope and search for him. A trail of broken twigs marks his descent down the slope of one ridge and straight off the edge of an even steeper one. I hurry to the top of the second slope and look down.

Rennie and his kayak are in a tree.

"Did you see that, Miss Vicki? Did you see?" The sapling he hit is bent down a few feet from the ground. Rennie throws both his long legs out of the craft and leaps to the forest floor. The tree springs upright. The kayak remains firmly lodged, now a good twenty feet above the ground.

Rennie, somehow completely unhurt, refuses to hear any talk of fishing the kayak down from its perch. That's his trophy, and that's where it will stay.

Henceforth, this part of my woods is known as Kayak Tree.

ॐ

Each new day draws me closer to my showdown in court, but no nearer to a solution. I keep myself plenty busy with my new routine: patrol our mountain by night, haul water with Alaric in the early morning, then snooze the daylight away.

After our water run, Gertie and I curl up together on Aunt Colleen's bed and sleep until late afternoon. As the shadows stretch out, I coffee up, make sure Gertie takes a long drink out of her water bowl, and then we're off on our nightly rounds.

That same hard-edged moon rolls above the ridge and leaks its cold light into my woods. We walk a zig-zag course downhill from the cabin, since every time the moonshiners have come, they've been on the downhill side. Gertie has no complaints about our new nighttime ramble. She wags her way from one scent to the next. I've got better eyes than hers; she's got the superior nose and ears. Between us, we're a force to be reckoned with.

I didn't count on it being so sweet out here at night, jogging along with my dog in the moonlight, warm late-summer air brushing past us, the dry forest sizzling with insect song.

Gertie and I go on full alert at the same time. We wait for the sound to come again. Faintly, up the hill from us, where the brush gives way to bare rock, comes the jangle of a bolt against metal pipe. Someone's tripped our alarm system. The still air brings a trace of whispered voices, far off to our left. In a clump of rocks, off the trail and above us, a stray flicker of a flashlight beam.

I tap Gertie's nose and whisper, "Shhh!" We creep silently toward the moonshiners.

We're still many paces away when two men tumble out of a

rock crevice and hurtle down the path toward us, the beams of their flashlights slicing wildly.

They're on a collision course with us. Seconds before they barrel into us, they see us, swerve to either side, and pass us by. Gertie wheels around on her hind legs and leaps forward to give chase, nearly yanking me from my feet. I brace my heels against the rocks and pull her back.

The two men run like animals in the moonlight, flailing, tripping, falling hard, scrambling to their feet, and charging on. They break from the tree line just ahead of us and pull up sharply. They've just come to the ridge above the water tower. They windmill their arms to keep from plunging over the side.

One man dives behind a fallen log. His buddy rushes to join him.

Then comes the explosion.

An express train of heat and light slams into us from behind. We're in the air, then we're tumbling toward the cliff edge. I slam hard against a rock. I instinctively grasp Gertie's rope in both hands as tight as I can. Gertie reaches the end of it and snaps back toward me with a yelp.

The bright flash is followed by a rain of yellow and orange sparks, then a cloud of dust and rock. I pull Gertie to me tightly, and crabwalk us both toward the shelter of a thick tree trunk.

Rocks the size of small cats thud all around us. I close my eyes, hold Gertie tight and wait for it to be over.

The mountainside is exhaling acrid black smoke. Red cinders swarm in thick, smoky beams of moonlight. My ears are ringing; I can't hear anything else. Gertie licks my face. I press my palm against my ear and it comes away bloody. Gertie leans on me, helping me to my feet. I run my hands over her body from muzzle to tail. She seems fine. I give myself a quick going-over. A few bruises, both ears out of commission, and a shallow gash to the head, but otherwise, okay.

A chemical, ashy scent clogs the air. I pick my way over smoking rubble and pass my flashlight over the rock face. The cleft of rock is gone. In its place is a charred gouge, a wound in the mountain's flesh, black and sooty.

As I approach the spot, the toe of my boot bumps against an object half buried in the dirt. I brush the debris aside and discover a bundle of six gray cylinders with red and white striped fuses, held together with electrical tape.

I shove the unused dynamite in my pocket and climb the rest of the way up to what's left of the rock cleft. What was a jutting outcrop of stone is now a shallow scoop. Its very shape speaks of the violence that was done to it. The wound in my mountain is deep. I reach my hand out to touch the ragged surface and pull it back in surprise.

My fingers are wet.

6

I rub my eyes with my sooty fingers and peer at the rock. A trickle of water dribbles out onto the ground. It's already making a muddy, ashen puddle. I'm standing in it.

The puddle overflows at one end then disappears beneath the dry leaves that blanket the forest floor.

I can't swallow. I can't inhale.

I can't possibly defend what I do next, but I do it just the same. I scrape up as much dirt as I can with my bare fingers and I pack the crevice with it until the flow is covered. I cover the puddle with ash, leaves, and rubble. I try to make it all look like the rest of the blast site.

Then I head back up to the cabin, wrap the unused bundle of dynamite in a gray T-shirt, climb onto Aunt Colleen's butcher-block table, and set the package on a rafter, in the shadow of one of the roof timbers. I wash the soot from my hands and face and change into a clean T-shirt.

When the Collier County sheriff's ATV pulls into my yard a half hour later, I tell him the story about hearing a noise and discovering the two men fleeing just as the blast went off. Except I leave out the part about finding the bundle of dynamite.

And the water.

✿

Althea keeps a pack of Pall Malls rolled up in the left sleeve of her green and white sun dress. An old-fashioned paper pack of matches rests just inside the plastic wrapper.

She and I sit in rockers on her porch. We each hold a steel bowl of shelled butter beans between our knees. Althea always gives part of her water ration to her vegetable garden. She has the only fresh produce for miles around.

We take handfuls of freshly picked beans from the bushel

basket on the table. With our thumbnails, we slip them from their shells as we talk. We drop the empty bean pods into a paper sack between us. Gertie snores loudly at my feet.

I've spent the afternoon tutoring Cooper's Forge kids in math, English, and geography. I've even started a few of them on what little high school French I can still remember. I've done this every Friday since I arrived. At this point, I'm in serious danger of falling in love with these kids.

Since Labor Day came and went, and Collier County public schools didn't re-open, I'm all the school these kids have now.

Summer has left Cooper's Forge, days grown shorter, shadows longer, nights colder. Sunlight falls, diamond-clear, all around us, no more haze or heat shimmers. The air pongs with the patchouli scent of dry leaves.

"We don't get no more color in the fall," Althea says slowly. "Before the rain stopped, this whole valley'd light up like it was on fire."

Althea unrolls her sleeve, retrieves a cigarette from the pack, lights it with a match, and re-rolls the whole bundle with a motion honed to perfection by time.

I haven't told Althea about the water on my land. I haven't told anyone. I don't know why. But the longer I go without saying anything, the harder it becomes.

"Your ear doing all right now?"

After the explosion, my left ear wouldn't stop bleeding. The townsfolk insisted I go to the hospital in Harrisonburg.

"It's on the mend. I can hear out of it, mostly."

Fridays on the porch with Althea. If she knew what I'd been keeping from her, could we still sit like this?

"And your court date?"

"In two weeks."

Ironic. When governments start to come apart, the schools go first. But the courts, they keep humming along.

"You got a plan, what you're going to say to that judge?"

"Well, I can prove I've been living on the land. That will make it harder for Steen to make the case that it should be given to him. Then it's just a matter of raising the money for the tax bill."

"Something will turn up. Always does. Your aunt Colleen, she'd say, It'll all turn out right in the end."

I could sell the water from my newfound spring—if it ever amounts to more than a trickle. But that would be the ultimate betrayal. A kick in the teeth to the closest I've ever had to family.

All at once I find myself asking, "Althea? Is there anything...I should know about Alaric?"

"Something in particular you want to know?"

"How long has he lived here?"

"Not long." In true Cooper's Forge fashion, Althea gives as little information as possible in response to a question. *Not long* could mean a few months or a few decades. Carl moved to the valley eight years ago and they still call him the new guy.

"Has Alaric got family anywhere?"

"Heard tell he's got some somewhere. A daughter, if I recollect."

I drop a bean pod onto the floor. "Is he...is he related to Aunt Colleen?"

"Not that I'm aware."

I'm trying to figure out what to ask her next, how to get to the information she must have, when she says, "He's told you his news, ain't he?"

"I haven't been able to help him these last few mornings because of my messed-up ear. It's been a little while since I've even seen him."

"That ain't no surprise. He's never been much of one to talk to nobody."

"He talks to me."

"That's why I figured you'd know."

"Know what?"

"His yield's dropping. His spring ain't producing like it used to."

Althea pauses to let the news sink in. I stare, unblinking, into my bowl of beans. This is bad. This is so, so bad.

"Pretty soon, he's going to have to choose between keeping

the town supplied and giving it away to them thieving lowlifes hanging 'round the Springs."

"I thought the sheriff routed them all out after the explosion?"

"He did. They come right back. Like cocka-roaches."

"Does he know why it's dropping?"

"You'd think it'd be the aquifer's tapped out. But Alaric don't think so. He thinks somebody else managed to tap into it. Someone lower down the mountain from his'n. If he's right, whoever it is ain't saying nothing about it, and sure as shinola ain't sharing it with any of us."

Guilt strikes a lightning bolt to my chest. Like thunder rolling, it travels down my spine. Why didn't I just tell these people about my spring the moment I found it? I still don't know. But I've kept my secret so long, how can I hurt them now by letting them know I've been holding out on them?

"Around here, honey"—Althea takes a drag from her cigarette and lets out the smoke in a long, gray-white gout—"we say don't nothin' stink for no reason."

I look down at my bowl again and discover I've been tossing the shelled beans into the paper bag and the shells into the bowl. Althea's noticed too.

☙

Gertie and I make a quick breakfast of cold ravioli straight from the can, then we set off for Alaric's.

Our woods are still cool even with the sun nearly overhead. Unseen insects all around us thrum out their last calls for the season, a sizzling crackle, like eggs in a frying pan. The forest has transformed from leathery green to brittle parchment. Facing their second autumn with no rain, these trees cling to their colorless leaves like a small child to a blanket.

The forest has changed and so have I. In Baltimore, the only muscles I had were the ones I built at the gym twice a week. Fake fitness. Now, my body's grown sinewy, like a hornbeam tree. I've fallen into a habit, at idle moments, of running my hands along the hard contours of my arms and legs, reveling in the shapes that hard work and rugged living have brought out in me.

This place is opening something in me. A seedling of an unknown Vicki that took root in this mountain has begun to unfurl. I hope this emergent Vicki is a me I can live with, because there's no putting her back.

Gertie's changed too. There's a lot more dog to her now, on top of those huge paws. Her dewlaps hang below her chin. She has her goofy moments, but more and more, she moves through the world with purpose.

Long before we come in sight of Alaric's homestead, the dogs are baying out a welcome. Gertie answers.

We find Alaric on the roof of his cabin. Through binoculars, he's watching a hawk turn lazy eights on the thermals where the sun strikes the ridge. He never waves or smiles when I arrive. If anything, it seems as though he was expecting me and I showed up late.

He swings down a ladder and joins me on the ground.

I start to repeat what Althea told me, about his spring running low.

"Come on," he says. "Something you need to see."

He leads me to the gate. When Gertie and the others try to follow us out, he waves them back. "We'll leave the dogs here."

We travel, not up toward his spring, but down to the dry riverbed, across its stretch of pebbly sand, and up the other side.

As I'm stepping onto the parched remains of the river, I'm reminded of Alaric's story. The Long Man, with his head in our mountain and his feet in the sea. If the river's gone dry, are we walking on his corpse?

The trail runs nearly vertical up this side of the river valley. We're hoisting ourselves up it with our hands, jagged black rocks biting our palms. The trail at last levels out, then T-bones another trail. Alaric turns to the left.

I follow along behind him, marveling at the view of my own land across the valley. I've never seen it like this before, objectively, from a distance. I can make out a few landmarks. The flat-topped gray-green slab I've come to think of as Picnic Rock, although we've never had a proper picnic there. Mercifully, the rocks that hold the spring are invisible from this trail.

I spot the toppled water tower leaning against the cliff face, where I made my first big mistake since arriving here. I realize we're coming upon Kelso Springs from the opposite side of the one I approached on that moonlit night when I came to get my dog back.

Alaric says, "Stay low. It's best if they don't see us."

He walks without making a sound, despite the twigs and gravel all along the path. I'm a herd of elephants by comparison. I try to mimic what he does: toeing the ground without setting weight on that foot, pressing down slowly, rolling onto the ball of his foot, and then onto the heel. Only when he's certain the step will make no noise, he lets his weight settle on it.

Now we're on a rock ledge directly above the Springs. We creep toward the edge of the cliff and look down.

At first, it all looks empty, derelict. Then one of the cottage doors creaks open and three children run out. One of them, the tallest, might be the girl who gave Gertie back to me. I can't tell for certain. They emerge, giggling, and then shush each other. They scamper like rabbits through the blond grass between cottages and then vanish from sight.

The longer I watch, the more signs of life I see. Between two of the cottages, a woman sits on the remains of a marble bench. I wonder if this is the same woman I've only seen in shadows, who appears every morning to help Alaric carry in the water.

On the moldering balcony rails, blankets hang, airing out, catching the rays of midday sun. Behind some of the cottages, pickup trucks sit, parked in shadows, barely visible. Trash piles heaped with debris that looks far too new. Sheets tacked across windows. Empty jerry cans tossed into the yard, as though awaiting collection and refilling. They've come to expect Alaric to make his daily rounds.

"There's…a lot more of them now."

Alaric fixes me with a long glance. His bushy white eyebrows disappear into the rim of his hat. I've learned the hard way how much he hates it when I waste perfectly good oxygen stating the obvious.

He points to a triangle of shadow beside one of the outbuildings. All at once, I realize what I took for a pile of logs is a woman in a dark hoodie, crouched, unmoving, and alert, with a rifle across her lap. Alaric points to another spot behind the rubble of a collapsed statue. A man sits with his back against a chunk of marble, idly flicking at the safety catch on his gun.

I spot the three children popping out of a different door, hop-skipping down another path to the next cottage. "They don't look much like moonshiners."

"We're all moonshiners now," Alaric grumbles, "unless we're lucky enough to own land over an aquifer."

"Alaric, if there's not enough water to give the town *and* to help these people—"

We catch sight of a plume of gravel dust rising from the road leading into the Springs. A battered camper, followed by a dented van and a stake-body pickup truck, pulls up in front of the main hotel. A sea of dusty faces stare out from the slats of the truck. A side door on the van slides open and a torrent of kids and dogs pour out. Adults follow last, stiffly unfolding themselves after the long ride.

So many people. So many kids. Cooper's Mountain must be drawing them like a beacon: the last remaining smudge of green in a brown, dying landscape.

"Alaric," I say, each syllable a razor blade to my conscience. "I'm so sorry. I can't possibly be sorrier. There's something *I* need to show *you*."

ॐ

Since I discovered it, I've been trying to build a catch-basin for my spring. I've hewed away at the rocky ground with the axe I found hanging by the hen house. I succeeded only in making a muddy divot in the ground.

When I lead Alaric to the spot and show him the damp wound in the flank of my mountain, he ignores my pathetic attempt at a catchment basin and shoves his hand directly into the crevice that produces the thready trickle.

He withdraws his dripping hand, sniffs it, and then sucks the water from it. He glances at me.

"Alaric, what should I do?"

"Not for me to decide."

"What can I possibly do with this tiny little dribble?"

"Tap into it, you might get a productive spring."

"I'm not Steen. I don't have money. I don't know how to do that."

Alaric pauses. He turns to look at me. "Have you learned nothing about the people of this town?"

He turns back to the path and walks away from me, up the hill.

7

Three water sources on this mountain: one dying, one not yet born, and one so full of life that it could keep the entire town and all the folks at Kelso Springs alive for years but locked away behind Steen's chain-link fence.

I spent all last night thinking it through while Gertie and I walked our nightly rounds. I awaken resolute. I know what I have to do.

As Gertie and I set off, I notice my empty porch. This is the first time since I landed on this perch in the mountains that Alaric hasn't brought me water. Maybe he's teaching me a lesson. Or maybe his spring is really that far gone.

Steen doesn't answer the first time I buzz the intercom. I know he's home, though. His stupid canary-yellow Lamborghini is here. I press the button again. And wait.

Gertie finds a stick to chew on.

At last, his voice comes through the speaker. "Go away, Vicki. We've got a court date pending."

"I'm not here about that," I yell into the speaker.

I wait. Gertie manages to snap her stick in two, then goes looking for a bigger challenge. I'm turning away to leave when the gate lurches into motion and slowly rolls open.

Steen waits for us at his front door. In a crisp black mariner's sweater, he still looks completely out of place on a West Virginia mountain. He looks at me in my grubby jeans and double layer of flannel shirts, then at Gertie, with her perpetual accessory of forest debris.

"Come in. Just leave your dog outside."

"We'll both stay out here."

"Suit yourself." He grins as if nothing has passed between us. "What can I do for you?"

"There's...water on my land."

"Yeah? I figured there must be. We're sitting over the same aquifer."

"I want to make a deal. I'll give you an easement to drill a well and tap the water on my land if you guarantee in writing the people in the town have the water they need."

"They've already got water."

"Not anymore. You heard about Alaric's source going dry?"

"Sorry, who?" He's checking his cell phone, which I know for a fact doesn't get a signal up here.

"Come on, Steen. These people are running out of time. My spring needs to be excavated before it can do anybody any good, and I can't afford it. You're the only hope they've got."

"I'll sell my water to them at half price. It's not like I haven't offered before."

"You know they don't have that kind of money."

"Seller's market, Vicki. If they need it bad enough, they'll find a way to afford it."

"That's disgusting."

"That's commerce." He flashes that shitty little grin that makes me feel like my soul has been bitten by a black widow. "I get something, they get something. It's fair. You know what's really disgusting? People who keep taking and taking, and never give anything back."

"I have no idea what you're talking about."

"Who paid the taxes on your land? Who's the only resident of Cooper's Forge who pays any taxes at all up here? Me. Yet the sheriff comes to your property when he's called. The post office is still open. Roads are still maintained. Fire department funded. You people are running around giving each other pound cakes and bushels of tomatoes. I keep life in Cooper's Forge going and what do I get? A spit in the eye."

This is going nowhere. I turn to leave, but he's not done.

"The first day you got here, Vicki, your very first day, remember? Who helped you out of that water tank? Who gave you a long, hot shower, fixed you up and brought you home?

All I asked in return was you keep an eye on things for me, but even that was too much for you to do."

Even though he's laying on his fruity breakfast-cereal voice, Gertie's not fooled. She sees my agitation, drops her stick, and comes to stand at attention by my side. Cooper's Forge born and bred; she knows nothing stinks without a reason.

"Then I offered to buy your land outright," Steen continues. "With the cash from the sale, you could have bought thousands of gallons of water for your rustic friends. But you wouldn't sell."

"I've changed my mind. I'll sell it to you right now." The words come flying out of my mouth without having consulted my brain first. "We can tell the judge we settled out of court. I'll sell at half price. A quarter. Just make sure the people in town have water."

"Vicki, that's not in my best interest. In two weeks, I'll have your land for nothing." He flashes a platinum-white smile. "And now I'm afraid I have to say good night." He steps inside and closes his door.

My insides are re-living my long fall into the water tank, the ice-water in my veins, the lurches in my belly. I stand on Steen's walkway, clenching my fists until my palms sting from the bite of my fingernails. But there's nothing else I can do except turn around and walk out of his compound.

As I pass through the gate, Steen's voice buzzes from the intercom. "When they start to die of dehydration, just remember you could have done something about it, and you didn't. It'll be on you, Vicki. All on you."

I walk in silence the whole way home. Gertie paces somberly beside me. My mood is her barometer.

I sit with Alaric on the rock that overlooks his cabin. He stitches a hole in a canvas tarp. His hands are never idle.

There's not enough water to fill the truck, but I've begun turning up again, just after four every morning, all the same.

We listen to the valley. Before I came to Cooper's Forge, I never knew how to hear different kinds of silence. This one is tense, turgid, as though it could burst at any second. The people at the Springs are thirsty. And angry. No more fruits to the sea.

I know what Alaric is planning. He's getting ready to go to Kelso Springs and tell them what's happened to his water.

"How do you think they'll take it? Why don't you let me come with you?"

He turns away and unspools another length of thread.

"You're going to take your dogs with you, at least?"

"Dogs are over at Carl's for the day." He's rolling his sewing kit into the canvas. I sense the conversation is coming to an end.

"How long have you lived up here, Alaric?" And when he doesn't respond, I try, "Where are you from, originally?"

Instead of getting pissed as I expect, he twists half his mouth into what someone with a good imagination might even call a grin. He taps the side of my boot with the toe of his.

"You tell the folks in town about your water?"

"It's hardly more than a trickle. I'm afraid to get their hopes up."

Out of the corner of my eye, I study his face. Not wrinkled exactly, but burnished, like a well-worn leather jacket. A tree I've learned to call hornbeam grows in my woods. Its branches display the same hard, sinewy twists as Alaric's arms. Yet, today, something about him seems frail.

"Feed my goats, city girl." He slides down from the rock and makes for the trail.

"Alaric?" I blurt suddenly. "Do you have a daughter?"

He stops and stiffens. Then without turning back to me, he slips off into the parched forest.

When I get back to my cabin, I kick off my boots and crawl into bed. I pull the quilt up over my head.

I'm like a tube of toothpaste in a vise grip, every ounce of me squeezed out, utterly spent. I have no more ideas, no more energy, no more will.

Some unknown river of time flows over me.

A while later, I hear the gnatty buzzing of an ATV engine growing louder, making its way up my side of the mountain. Irony of ironies, when I lived in Baltimore, I could be anonymous whenever I wanted, and when I slid the bolt to my apartment door, I could count on being left alone. Now here, on the side of a West Virginia mountain, where you'd think there'd be hardly anyone around, I can't get a moment's peace.

Cool Breeze pulls up in my yard and knocks on my door. Without waiting for an answer, he opens it. "Come on with me, now, Vicki Truax. We've called a town meeting."

We meet in the basement of the Cooper's Forge Baptist Church. A crowd has gathered around a back table, ladling something steamy into bowls and filling plastic tumblers with tea.

I scan the room and recognize Mack and Tippy and their three kids. There's Tom, Carl, Happ, and that old sourpuss, Early. Breeze's wife Bright, Lila McAphee. People I remember from Althea's, folks whose kids I tutor. Even Bill and Newt, Steen's goons, sit on the bottom steps, staring into their bowls. But there are even more people here, residents of Cooper's Forge who I haven't yet met. This must be an all-hands meeting. I don't see Alaric, though.

Susan appears from somewhere behind me, squeezes my arm, and presses a bowl into my hands. "Here you go, honey, come sit over here." She leads me to a folding chair, one of a few dozen all set in a double circle.

The bowl that's now burning my fingers is full of chicken and dumplings, with a bright yellow square of cornbread stuck in it. Susan plops a spoon into my bowl, sets a glass of sweet tea in my empty hand, pats my shoulder, and moves off to help get the rest of the crowd settled.

The tea tastes of my mountain: crisp, like wet stone after a rainstorm, probably brewed on somebody's sunny front porch.

The meeting doesn't begin until Althea arrives in her green and white sundress and an ivory shawl, squeezes the hands that are offered her, and sits in the place of honor.

The chatter quiets.

"Well, now," Althea begins, perusing the faces around the circle. "Looks like we're all here. Shame it ain't under better circumstances."

A murmur of assent rumbles through the room.

"I 'spect by now you all heard about what happened to Alaric. Them people at Kelso, they beat him pretty bad."

A breathy sound leaps out of my throat. I throw a hand over my mouth. The room fills with gasps and whispers. This news is a surprise to more than just me.

"He's in the hospital down to Harrisonburg. That's about all I know. Anyhow, there's more I got to say…" She pauses and waits for the murmurs to subside. "Y'all know Alaric's spring ain't going to keep us going much longer. So, we got to work out where our water's going to be coming from. If we can't, we got no choice but to move on."

"That McMasters fella, maybe we can get a judge to force him to give us some from his well."

"Already tried."

"What other choice have we got?"

Amid the back-and-forth, I lower my head and raise my hand. I wait until they notice. Althea says, "You got something you want to say, Miss Vicki?"

I rise from my chair. I will my voice not to crack. "You all don't deserve to be given false hope. But I owe it to you to let you know, I've found some water on my land. It's small. It's not nearly enough to replace what Alaric was giving you. But you have a right to know it's there."

I look around the room, expecting anger and judgment, waiting for calls of, Why didn't you tell us before? But they're silent, waiting grimly for me to finish what I have to say.

So, I continue. "But you all probably also know, in less than a month, Steen McMaster's likely going to own my piece of land.

I just wanted you all to know I'd do anything in the world if I could help. But I'm out of options."

I sit back down as the room fills with voices. Lost in my shame, I barely feel the pats on my back. Becky and Cindy Lyons come up and throw their arms around me.

The conversation swirls all around me. Just as I'm wondering whether I can slip out of the room unnoticed, the talk subsides and I look up to find all eyes on me.

"It's settled, Miss Vicki," Carl says. "We're coming to court with you week after next. And, by damn, if there's water underneath your land, we'll help you get to it."

I leave Gertie at Althea's, playing with her two Scotty dogs. Breeze drops me off behind his store so I can retrieve my car.

"Me and Bright can come with you, if you like," he offers.

"That's kind of you, Breeze. I think I need to go on my own."

Breeze takes my hand in his and pats it. "We'll see you tomorrow, then."

I drive out of Cooper's Forge, past drier, deader towns. In one borough, I pass a rectangle of shriveled grass and hedges, with abandoned basketball courts and jungle gyms, bearing the name *Christmas City Park*. Either these folks keep the holiday spirit year-round, or Bright's family name holds some weight around here.

I drive to Harrisonburg in silence. I find Alaric's hospital room and enter quietly. In the low florescent light, I study him a long while before I'm even certain I'm looking at the right person. He's frail and deflated, bandaged, breathing from an oxygen mask. Plastic tubing protrudes from a vein in one arm. So far out of his element, he can't be mistaken for a young man.

I draw a breath and take out a heavy book from my knapsack. One of the few textbooks I've held on to since college: *World Mythology*. I flip to the first page of several I've book-marked with dry autumn leaves from my mountain.

"So, Alaric, the Sawa people of Cameroon believe water is full of spirits. They're called *jengu*. They're good luck. And beautiful too."

A muscle at the corner of his eye twitches. His breathing remains shallow.

"The ancient Norse believed the sea itself was a person. A giant named Aegir. The Greeks considered water to be a sacred drink…"

I read through every leaf-marked page. Then I sit with him a long while. He doesn't open his eyes.

In the dark, I make the drive back to my mountain without the slightest evidence that he even knew I was there.

I wake in the morning to the deep, throaty thrumming of a diesel engine. Something huge is making its way up the mountain.

I chug down yesterday's leftover coffee and step outside to watch a massive flatbed truck lurching its way up a dirt track that's not nearly big enough for it. Townsfolk on ATVs accompany the truck fore and aft, like tugboats bringing in an ocean liner.

I expect the flatbed will carry backhoes and drills, tools to excavate my spring. What it has instead is chain-link fence. Massive rolls of half-rusted fencing, stacks of long poles twice my height.

Several of the ATVs are towing utility carts stacked high with barbed wire.

Breeze pulls up and hops off his ATV. "Morning, Vicki Truax."

"Where'd all this come from?"

"Oh, we've been busy. The chain link comes from Little League fields in a bunch of towns. It's not like they need them now."

True. Nobody plays sports anymore. Fear of dehydration ruins a lot of fun.

"And the barbed wire?"

"Every farm in this area's got loads of that."

Happ hands me a pair of thick brown leather gloves and we set to work hauling chain link, poles, and wire down to the site of my spring. Althea, Lila, and four other older women set up a camp kitchen with an enormous kettle, iron grates, and enamel coffee pots. They keep coffee brewing, ham and eggs frying, and cornbread baking from dawn to dusk. My Friday tutoring students run back and forth filling tin mugs from jerry cans, keeping everyone watered.

Four days later, the woods around my spring looks like a concentration camp. Towering chain-link fence rings the area, with enough room inside for heavy equipment to move. Barbed wire tops the fence and a thick coil of it runs around the base.

Gertie and I don't sleep in our cabin anymore. We've got a gray and blue tent inside the fence. We have company every night. Tom and Susan, Tippy, Mack, and their three kids, Breeze, though never with his wife, and sometimes a few others pitch tents alongside mine and keep vigil.

On the fifth day, the excavation begins. The townsfolk dig a deep hole downslope from the water source and line it with stones. Then they begin, carefully, to chip away at the gray-green rock around the spring itself.

Days pass in a flurry of activity. At night, I lean back on a camp chair and close my eyes, pretending, for a moment, things are back to the way they were.

The folks living in the Springs seem emboldened by their attack on Alaric. Or else they're simply growing desperate. Most nights, some unwary foot triggers my pipe-and-bolt alarm system.

One night, after dozing off in my chair, I awaken to see faces staring in at me from the other side of the fence, otherworldly in the flashlight beams.

I crawl inside my tent, zip myself in, hug Gertie close to me, and weep into her furry, rumpled neck.

My place has begun to look like Steen's.

❧

At daybreak, I slip through the chain link and retrieve my cell phone, which hasn't had a charge in months. Gertie and I set off down the mountain.

The woods themselves seem tensed for calamity. Not a puff of wind, no creaking branch, not even the patter of leaf-fall. I've grown used to the occasional creak and moan of a dead tree toppling, but today they've all chosen to keep their grasp on the Earth. The mountain is waiting.

My little green Chevy still sits at the ready behind Christmas General Store. It starts right up. Gertie takes up her post riding shotgun and we drive to the top of the hill outside of town, where, if I park just right, I can sometimes get a signal. I plug the phone cord into my cigarette lighter and wait for it to pick up enough of a charge to place a call.

While I wait, a caravan of three pickup trucks passes us. The beds of the trucks are filled with people, glassy eyed with desperation. I wonder if they're all headed for Kelso Springs.

My phone is charged. I place the call.

"Baby girl? Is that you?"

"Hey, Thora." All at once I'm sobbing. I yank the phone away from my ear and clap my hand over my mouth so she won't hear.

"Honey, where are you?"

I pull in one deep breath and force my body to behave itself. "I'm here. At the mountain. Well, near it."

"You okay?"

"Yeah. I'm good. Just wanted to hear your voice."

"Are you safe? You got water?"

"Yeah, yeah. We found a spring on my land. Me and this one other guy, we're the only two people with water in the whole place."

"Oh, honey. You need to get out of there. They'll kill you for it."

"It's okay. Really. I can take care of myself. And I got the whole town looking out for me. How…how's Toronto?"

"Toronto's fine. It's you I'm worried about. You still got that ugly-ass car?"

"I'm sitting in it now."

"You got money for gas?"

Yeah, a little. But I can't leave right now."

"Girl, you better get out of there while you still can."

In my mind, I'm slamming the car door, locking us in, and peeling out for Toronto. But I say into the phone, softly, "I just needed to hear your voice, is all."

8

It's court day. I root through my cardboard boxes of clothes until I find a charcoal-gray suit I used to wear to the office. I lay it out on the bed. It looks as out of place in Aunt Colleen's cabin as a poodle running with a wolf pack.

I heat water in the kettle, take a one-gallon bath, eat a bowl of cold applesauce, and get dressed. The soft linen is foreign on my skin after months of jeans and flannels.

I step out into the eerie stillness. Susan climbs up from the spring encampment, puts her arms around me and says, "You'll be fine. Everything will be just fine."

I send Gertie off to stay with her at the spring for the day.

Breeze arrives on his ATV and gives me a lift to my car. And then I'm on my way to the court.

The brick walkway leading to the Collier County Courthouse is studded here and there with marble inserts bearing the names of donors. On more than one, I read the last name *Christmas*. Bright's family must be an institution in this corner of the world.

In the cool marble foyer of the court building stands a table with a dispenser of water and paper cups. My throat is rawhide; I won't even try to force water down it.

I'm the first to arrive in the court room. My friends from Cooper's Forge are not here. I sit alone amid wood paneling and navy-blue carpet, wondering how it will feel once I've officially had my land taken from me. It's impossible to know because the part of me that feels things has gone into hiding. Got the hell out of Dodge. Left no forwarding address.

Steen and a sleek bearded fellow in a dove-gray suit enter and take their seat at the plaintiff's table. He flashes his chromium smile in my direction. My guts squirm.

It's not until the call of "all rise" comes and the judge enters that the ice hits my veins.

This judge is a dour fellow with a corn-fed huskiness common to these parts. He has a comical amount of silky gray hair on the sides of his head and none on the top. He scratches at his neckline as he sits, opens a folder on his desk, and leafs through it.

The bailiff commands us to be seated. We wait as the judge shuffles papers. He looks over to Steen and raises his eyebrows. He looks over at me and furrows them.

He directs us to speak our names. He reads the facts of the case. He asks Steen to state his complaint.

"Your Honor, I've been caretaker of the land adjacent to mine for the last several years, ever since its owner abandoned care of it. Rather than allow a delinquency, I've paid the property taxes with my own money." Steen indicates me with a jerk of his head. "The owner of record, who inherited the land, took up residence on the land a few months ago, but did not offer to reimburse me. Nor has she paid the taxes she owes to the county. If it pleases the court, I move that I be granted ownership of the land for which I've taken responsibility."

The judge scratches at his neckline and says, "An active spring has recently been discovered on this property, is that correct?" He's addressing this question to Steen, and not to me. This can't be a good sign.

"Yes, Your Honor. I have the funds and the equipment to develop the spring into a productive source. But Miss Truax is unemployed and has no source of income and, in fact, during her four months' tenure on the land, she had done nothing to improve it."

"Miss Truax?" The judge barely looks at me. "Please tell me why you're here today."

My voice comes out of my mouth robotically. Someone else's voice. Someone else's mouth. "Your Honor, I inherited the land on Cooper's Mountain from my aunt, Colleen Bolivar. It was in her will and it transferred legally to me. I wasn't informed of any taxes owed, but if you'll give me a few months' extension, I'll find a way—"

The judge waves me into silence. He draws a long breath, still never fully resting his eyes on me. "Miss Truax, if these were ordinary times, the court might consider leniency. But in this part of the country, we're in a fight for our lives here. If there's water to be had on your land, that represents lives we can save. And if you don't have the means—"

I'm already losing. He's made up his mind. My land's about to be taken from me.

All at once, the words come pouring out.

"If Steen McMasters gets a hold of that water, the people of Cooper's Forge won't get a drop of it!" Squeakily, I add, "Your Honor." I jab a thumb in Steen's direction. "He's been selling off water from his own land at eighty, ninety-some dollars a gallon. Never given so much as a cup of water to the people of my town. You let him have my spring too, there's a whole community thrown into crisis!"

Steen rises and says coolly, "Your Honor, if I may..." I could smack him for sounding so calm. "I think you'd agree with me that even in the middle of a drought, the law still stands. A man can still do what he wants with his own property. Isn't that so? And besides, Miss Truax is not telling you the whole truth when she says the residents never get any of my water. She herself has tasted quite a bit of it, thanks to my generosity."

"That's not the point!" My fists are balled so tightly I can feel my nails digging into my palms. Jeez, Vicki, what *is* the point? "The thing is, people out there in that valley are only a few days away from dying of thirst, every day. We can't just turn on a municipal tap or line up at a water truck. All we have is the water in that mountain!"

The judge rubs his brow. "Sit down, please. Miss Truax, Mr. McMasters. We may be in the middle of the apocalypse here, but in my court, we're still going to maintain order."

The courtroom door squeaks open and a woman from the clerk's office enters. She crosses directly to the judge, lays a paper before him, and whispers something to him. They speak in hushed tones.

The judge now looks at me full-on. "I have before me a receipt from the clerk of the court that says this debt has been paid in full. This morning. This here is a check to Mr. McMasters for the full amount of the funds he paid to the county on behalf of Ms. Bolivar's estate."

Steen is on his feet again. "Your honor, the spring will still go untapped if—"

The courtroom door opens again, and in comes Early in a brown wool suit, followed by Happ, Carl with Lila on his arm, Tom and Susan, Tippy and Mack, Breeze, and just about every other adult resident of Cooper's Forge. All in their Sunday clothes. The last one in the door is Althea herself, walking with two wooden canes, slowly making her way up the aisle. She stops at the gate just beyond the last row of benches.

The judge's disdainful expression melts to something inscrutable. Is that respect? It might even be fear. He nods stiffly to the indomitable woman standing at the center of his courtroom.

He says to Althea, "Good to see you again, Your Honor."

Oh. The wooden hammer in the glass case on her living room wall. Not a crab mallet. A gavel.

"Jacob," she replies. Then she turns and looks at me. She winks and nods, as if to say, Go on, girl.

I take a moment to compose myself, but my hands shake anyway. In a voice that wouldn't frighten a flea, I begin, "Your Honor, my neighbors in Cooper's Forge are helping me excavate my spring. Whatever water we get, I'll share with the town at no charge. I'll put that in writing if you like."

The judge steps out of the courtroom. Long minutes drag by. No one stirs. I can't even hear them breathing.

We rise. The judge returns. We sit.

"Miss Truax, in light of these additional circumstances, I believe we have a duty to uphold your claim to that land. The court finds in favor of the defendant." Before I can draw a breath, the judge gestures to me. "Would you approach the bench, please?"

I rise onto knees that threaten to wobble if I don't keep them in check, and step toward the judge. As I draw closer, he leans over to his clerk and exchanges a few words with her that I can't make out. She thumbs through a file folder on her desk and hands him a stapled set of papers.

Now I'm standing in front of him. He leans over to me and says quietly, "Miss Truax, strictly speaking, I'm not allowed to give you legal advice, but if I were, I might suggest you and your neighbors consider filing a claim for eminent domain. That'll protect it from anyone who might try to take it from you in the future. In ordinary times, a claim like that wouldn't fly. But hell, there's nothing ordinary about these times."

My legs have turned to spaghetti. I try to remember how to breathe.

"Now, I'm not allowed to give you forms," the judge says, "but if I just happened to drop them on the floor, and you just happened to pick them up, well…"

He holds the papers out over the edge of his desk, drops them practically at my feet, and says, "Oops."

The judge and Althea exchange another wordless communication, the kind that passes between mentor and protege. He gives me one last nod. "Have a nice day, Miss Truax."

I scoop up the forms from the floor and scurry back to my table. The townsfolk rise and he leaves the courtroom. I will myself not to look at Steen, but I can't stop myself from glancing over at him. He's on his feet, staring at me, his eyes primitive and cold, like the ones on that snake in my cabin rafters.

Susan helps me fill out the forms and return them to the clerk. As we pass a wall full of commemorative plaques, she squeezes my arm and taps at a mahogany-and-gold rectangle with the etching of a face I recognize. The name under it reads The Honorable Althea Butler, Collier County Circuit Court, 1992 – 2024.

"She trained up more'n half the judges in this county," Susan whispers behind her hand.

And then we're all filing out into the parking lot.

Hugs, handshakes, and smiles all around, and me in the middle, clamping my jaws shut over the sobs that keep knocking at the back of my throat. I won't, no I won't, let these good people, with hearts of gold and bones of iron, see me break down in tears.

I take up the rear of a victory procession headed back to Cooper's Forge, the townsfolk honking and yelling victory whoops out the window.

I don't deserve them.

Without either of us saying a word about it, Susan and I fall into the routine of doing chores together. With an entire city's-worth of people all around, I'd have never thought to call a girlfriend over to do laundry with me. It's not the work that brings me so much joy; it's the sharing of it. The easy laughing and chatting and basking in one another's presence.

Every other Monday, it's laundry. In Baltimore, I'd clean my clothes with white vinegar or rub them down with body wipes if I had them. In Cooper's Forge, we accomplished our waterless clothes-washing by alternating techniques: one week, turning them inside-out and fluffing them with baby powder, the next, laying them in the dry grass on a sunny hillside to bake under a cloudless sky.

The November air carries a chill but the sun shines summer-bright. I leave Gertie to play with Susan's old red and white hound and we push our way through the dry saplings until we emerge onto a grassy, rock-strewn slope. The soundtrack to the laying-out of dirty clothes is our light banter. Time flows gently when Susan's around.

I'm in mid-laugh when my eye registers something at the edge of the woods. Before I can work out what I'm seeing, a tremor runs through my gut. A person stands there, not moving, eyes on us, and a shotgun in both hands.

I'm about ninety percent sure this is the woman who met Alaric each morning to haul water for the people in the Springs. She seems made of twigs and bark, dark, creased, and gnarled. A yellow cloth wraps her head tightly. The gun rests in her hands like it grew there. I wonder, when they beat Alaric into a coma, did she join in the beating, or did she try to stop it? They were friends, sort of, or at least acquaintances; she'd try to save him. Wouldn't she?

I think what's swimming up my spine is called fear of the unknown. But it's just a fellow human, maybe a future friend if I give her half a chance, says the part of me whose first impulse is always to whistle into the wind. But that chill between my shoulder blades begs to differ.

Ah well, what the hell. I raise my hand in a wave.

"Vicki, quit!" Susan has her head down, pretending to study an oil stain on Tom's overalls. "Don't look at her. Don't say nothin' to her."

"Who—"

"She's from Kelso Springs, them people that robbed you and jumped poor old Alaric."

"You know her?"

"She ain't Cooper's Forge," Susan hisses. "That's enough to know."

I wait until Susan's busy with one of Cindy's lime-green jumpers. I sneak another look at the tree line.

But the woman with the gun is gone.

I'm sitting at Althea's kitchen table with Becky, the less academically inclined of Mack and Tippy's girls. Tutoring days are now three times a week, by the request of the Coopers' Forge kids themselves, believe it or not.

"You read the type of sentence," I tell her, "and I'll give you an example."

"Okay. Declarative."

"I love Zambonis."

"What's a Zamboni?"

Her mom asked me work with her especially on grammar and internet research. Her adoptive mom. The girls' biological parents were killed in a highway crash seven years ago. Tippy and Mack, already raising Rennie, adopted them. There are no orphans in Cooper's Forge.

I've got my old work laptop charged and running in her sitting room—Althea has a gas generator that can provide electricity to the house for a few hours—and I've even managed to rout an internet connection through my phone.

"In-ter-rogative."

"Would you like to see my Zamboni?"

"What *is* a Zamboni?" Becky giggles.

Althea's adding cups of sugar to a steel mixing bowl, making a pudding out of the nastiest fruit I've ever tasted. Something called a persimmon. They looked festive on their tree, reds and oranges, waxy and bright, against the leafless black branches. One of the only trees left bearing anything we could harvest. But after we picked them, I tasted one: so mouth-puckeringly bitter, I doubted even Althea could make something edible from it.

"Next," I prompt Becky.

"Exclamatory."

"Wow, look at that Zamboni!"

"Come on, Miss Vicki. What *is it?*"

"One more."

"Im-perative."

"Don't touch my Zamboni!"

"Arrgggh!" Becky shakes a fist at me. "Tell me!"

"See my computer over there? Go look it up. Remember how I showed you?"

She flounces off to do her research.

It's been three weeks since we filed the paperwork to claim imminent domain over Steen's well. I check the mail every day. Still nothing.

Althea's smiling at me. "Teaching's your cup of tea." She

beats five eggs together and folds them into the foul brown-black mix of mashed persimmons.

"I never thought I'd like teaching."

"You mean to say you never taught nobody before?"

"This is my first time."

"You're good at it. Must run in the family."

She punches a hole in a can of milk and beats it into the mix. No one has fresh milk anymore. Lactating animals drink too much water. All of the farmers around Cooper's Forge have already butchered their livestock, rather than watch them die of thirst.

Nobody's slaughtering their dogs, though. These days, a supply of water makes you vulnerable to attack, unless dogs are guarding it. Better than a gun: nobody can ever use your dog against you. When all other animals have become a luxury, we keep our dogs close.

Becky calls from the front parlor, "Miss Althea, someone's coming up your drive."

Althea's two Scotties launch themselves out of their basket, out the screen door, and down the steps to yap at the battered beige camper van pulling up to the house.

"Want me to go see what they want?"

Althea dusts off her apron. "No, child. I'll take care of it." She walks outside, down the steps, and over to the camper van. The driver is rolling down his window. He's curly haired, fresh-faced. Younger than me. Three dark-haired girls peek over his shoulder.

"You're on private property, son."

"I just need some water. A couple gallons. Whatever you can spare."

"Can't spare none."

"Can you at least give my girls a cup of water to drink?"

"That I'll do," Althea says slowly, "then you git on out of here."

"Yes, ma'am."

Althea returns to the kitchen, and I help her fill four tumblers with water from her kitchen jerry can. We carry them out to the family in the van. While they're drinking, she returns to the kitchen for a tin of biscuits and a jar of pickled bean salad. She hands them to the driver.

"That's to get you on the road. We ain't got enough for our own here. Can't help you. You ride on out of here and keep going. Hear?"

"Thank you, ma'am."

The camper van pulls away. We return to the kitchen and Althea puts her casserole of persimmon nastiness into the oven.

"That was nice of you, giving those folks food and water."

"Wasn't the least bit nice. I was following orders."

"Who ordered you to do that?"

Althea points to the polished rosewood cross that hangs above her kitchen clock.

"He did."

Walking dehydrates me, and none of us can afford that now. But sometimes, I feel the need to hike back up the mountain after a day at Althea's. On foot, I can listen to these woods, read their mood, take their temperature, in a way I can't do on the back of Breeze's ATV.

Before the rain stopped, I expect a walk in the woods this time of year must have meant shushing through piles of autumn leaf-fall. But these trees won't relinquish their shriveled leaves. Like mothers grieving stillborn infants, they hold those desiccated little bodies close.

I hear the tell-tale cracking of a tree about to topple. I pause because these woods are so full of echoes, I can't be sure all at once how close by it may be. Uphill and to my right, a tall, slender pine starts it spiraling descent to the forest floor. Trees cry out as they fall, in anguished, nearly human voices. The pine ensnares a few of its sisters on its tumble and takes them down with it. They crash, and bounce, and lie still.

More trees are falling nowadays. Many more than when I

first arrived. I suppose two summers without rain is more than most of them can take. And few have roots deep enough to sip the aquifer. I wonder if there will be enough left alive to green up this mountain in the springtime.

Long before I'm anywhere near home, Gertie's joyful bark rings out. She knows I'm inbound. I've been leaving her with the work crew at the spring every day because her keen ears and nose alert them if anyone's snooping around.

Early, Susan, Tom, Lila, and Breeze hurry up to the fence when they see me. They're beaming. Some of them, I've never even seen smile before.

"Miss Vicki," says Tom, "it's with great pleasure that I announce: you got a working spring."

"And a reservoir," Susan adds.

"Come on. We'll show you."

They lead me through the fence and to the spring. I hear it before I see it: that silver swishing of water onto rock. What was once a trickle from a crack has been widened into a musical little stream. The splashing droplets scent the air with minerals. Water gushes into a stone basin the size of a deep bathtub. The basin has a hinged wooden lid that fits snug overtop to keep out bugs and leaves.

At the foot of the basin is something I take to be a faucet. They have Alaric's water tank and trailer parked near it, with a hose attached. The tank is filling, slowly.

"It's beautiful, guys. How long will it take to fill the tank?"

"That's what we don't know yet," says Tom, his smile vanishing. "We were using three of these tanks a week when Alaric was bringing it. If it don't get full over a twenty-four-hour period, it ain't enough to keep the town going."

Susan adds, "And that's just accounting for drinking. That's with no bathing, or cooking, or anything for gardens."

"What about some for the folks in the Springs?" I ask.

"Who gives a pile of horse shit about them?" Early thunders. "They put one of our own in the hospital. They can dry up and blow off to hell!"

"Come on, you all," Susan soothes. "Can't we discuss this another time? We got Vicki's spring going. Tonight should be for celebrating."

No one tries to argue with that.

An hour later, Picnic Rock is finally getting used for picnicking. We set up one of Cindy's contraptions and hook it to its battery. Soon, we're filing tin plates with ham and beans, fried potatoes, those toothsome biscuits Cooper's Forge is famous for, and, from a jar, a relish I'm still a little wary of, which my neighbors call chow-chow.

I get my first sip of genuine Appalachian moonshine. I go back for a second taste. And a third. Half an hour later, all is right with the world.

Tom says, "Anybody's got a source on their land gets to name it, Miss Vicki. What'll you call yours?"

I'm thinking about Alaric's story of the river as a long, slim, sinuous man, his head resting in the mountains, his feet paddling in the sea. If he lays his head on Cooper's Mountain, that makes my little clump of land his pillow.

"The Long Man's Pillow," I say confidently. Then I realize how ridiculous it sounds.

Happ scrunches his face in confusion.

Early spits in the dust.

"What in the heck kinda name—" Tom begins, until his wife gives him a sharp dig in the side with her elbow.

"You just told her she can name it whatever she wants," Susan says defiantly. "So that's what we're gonna call it: The Long...what's it again, honey?"

I do my best to recreate the story Alaric told me. Lots of polite nods all around.

We sit on folding chairs in a circle, sipping our drinks, watching the night shadows rise out of the valley and devour the light. The sky turns that singular shade of turquoise that belongs to late-autumn nights. The air itself is clear as the moonshine in my cup. We take turns spotting stars as they emerge. In short order, there are far too many to count.

When the turquoise has turned to deep teal, then to navy blue, I spot a hazy, pinkish-yellow smear of light cutting across the sky.

"Guys. What is that?"

"That? That's the Milky Way, Miss Vicki."

"You're pulling my leg."

"Serious. That's why they call it the Milky Way, honey." Happ pats my hand. "Looks like someone done upset their milk pail all across the sky."

"That can't *be* the Milky Way, Happ. We're *in* the Milky Way."

Whatever it is, I can't take my eyes off it. Here I am with friends, on my land, with a sky full of more stars than a girl could ever need in a lifetime. I have a full belly, a dog snoozing at my feet, and a jar of homemade liquor in my hand.

I drift into a sleep woven out of mountain air and moonshine. Vicki Truax. Guardian of the Long Man's Pillow.

I sleep in my camp chair with Gertie's head resting on my feet, my face turned upward to the stars, and the universe rolling by overhead. Someone drapes a sleeping bag around me and tucks in the edges. Somebody sets a jug of water in arm's reach in case I wake up cotton-mouthed during the night.

In the limnal sleep-but-not-sleep that happens to me when I spend a night outdoors, I'm aware that my friends haven't left me alone. Susan, Tom, and Breeze are in sleeping bags nearby.

I've never known anything as delicious as waking up to the sunrise. Taking a few hours to cross from my inner world to the waking one. Dawning with the sun. The first cold glow on the horizon. Then pink. Then a ray of golden warmth. Then silhouettes become moving figures, then people I recognize. And then I smell coffee brewing.

When at last I'm ready to go to full-awake, I open my eyes to find Tom, kneeling on his haunches before me, holding out a tin cup of steaming black coffee. He's minus his usual, easy smile.

"Morning, Vicki. I wish I had better news for you."

I take the cup and down a few swallows. "What's the matter, Tom?"

"I checked the tank first thing this morning. It's not filling as fast as we'd hoped."

"Is there enough? For everyone in town?"

"Just barely. We'll have to ration a bit. We'll survive, but it ain't going to be plentiful."

"What about the people in the Springs?"

"Ain't nothing we can do for them."

"There's families there now. Little kids."

"They ain't kin, Vicki. Nor neighbors. They're strangers."

"Weren't you the one who said nobody had a right to withhold water from his fellow man?"

"I was talking about when there's enough to go around."

I cup my face in my hands. I remember getting a look at Mr. Rosen before the coroner took him away. I know what dying of thirst looks like. Now I imagine the little girls I saw running like rabbits from cabin to cabin, how they would look gasping out their last breaths on those dank cabin floors, succumbing to Mr. Rosen's fate.

"Vicki?" Tom calls from somewhere outside my cupped hands. "I wasn't...I wasn't talking about you. I wasn't talking about this. I was talking about Steen."

Right. Steen. I take my hands away from my face.

"What was it you said? A deed only means something in ordinary times?"

"Something like that."

I look out across the gray valley, and as far into it as I can see. The light's rolling swiftly down the mountain slopes, but it hasn't landed there yet.

"I've checked the mail. Every day. No word from the courthouse on our eminent domain papers. It's only a matter of time before those folks down there get desperate enough to come up here and try to take our spring by force. You know it and I know it."

"You're right. We been thinking about that for a couple weeks now."

"But we're not the ones with more water than we need. Steen is."

"Yeah. But do they know that?"

"Tom, I think I know what we need to do."

"What?"

"I think we need to go down there to the Springs and call for a parlay."

9

The whole morning goes to trying to convince the rest of the folks to head down to Kelso Springs on a peaceful errand. Early is dead set against it. No surprise there. He thinks we should rout them all out like they used to do before.

"Send 'em packing," he growls. "Let 'em find their water somewhere else. We ain't got none to spare."

This sounds more than halfway reasonable to me. Maybe we should do it Early's way. Or maybe we should go in tough, offer them a choice: Hit the road. Or help us liberate all that water Steen's been sitting on.

They must surely see sense in this. Especially if we bring them a peace offering. A couple jerry cans of water. But that's when I begin to shudder.

Because that's exactly what Alaric was doing when they beat him.

It's noon when we've finally settled it. We fill four ten-gallon cans and load them onto Breeze's ATV cart. We leave the dogs and the guns at camp. We walk into the Baths by the main road.

December without rain is no longer the way we once knew it. No thrill of frost, no tantalizing snow-clouds. The sun beats down fiercely, sucking away moisture from our bodies. We're muzzy-headed and miserable long before we come in view of the dilapidated resort.

As we approach, we take in the sight of dozens of people standing close together in the grass beside the main building. They murmur softly. They could be singing. Their heads are bowed, somber. This might be a Sunday worship service. Only, it's not Sunday. A tall man stands on a stack of packing pallets before the group. He cradles a small bundle wrapped in a sheet.

All at once, it hits me. This isn't a prayer service. It's a funeral.

The crowd hears our approach and glares at us.

I raise my hand in what I hope will be seen as a gesture of apology. I gesture to the townsfolk behind me to back up. The whole cavalcade of us walks backward down the gravel road, around the bend and out of sight.

"Now what?" grumbles Early.

"Now we wait," I say. "We caught them at a bad time. Let them finish burying their child."

We sit irritably, waiting in scratchy, waist-high grass.

"When it used to rain, a spot like this would be a haven for ticks," Susan comments. But no one picks up the thread of conversation.

We wait a while longer, then we send Cool Breeze running up the road. He reports back that they're finishing up.

Our little delegation is on the move again. This time, they're expecting us. A phalanx of armed men stands across the entrance to the Springs.

I feel the group behind me begin to waver, but I keep moving forward. I've done this before. Alone.

I stop before the line of men. "We'd like to talk with you folks. I think we can help each other."

I whisper to Breeze to bring up the water. He drives his ATV to the front of the line and displays the jerry cans.

One of the men turns and heads for the main building. This could be a good sign. Shooting us: that would be a not-good sign.

The man returns. The guards talk among themselves, then they step aside.

We're moving down the main road in between the cottages, heading for the hotel. We pass the little place amid the tall blond grass where the group held their funeral. A small dusty rectangle of mounded earth rests there now, crowned with river pebbles, stand-ins for the flowers that no longer bloom in this part of the world. Amid the tall dry grass, I catch sight of another grave, and another, and still more, carefully adorned with round black and yellow pebbles.

For the first time, I'm fully seeing Kelso Springs, not from an antique postcard, nor looking down from a cliffside, nor in moonlit half-shadow. Like an elderly dowager in declining health, the elegance and dignity of the place clings to it, despite the moldering wood and peeling paint.

Children peer out of windows. Women and men appear in doorways. Walking behind me, the townsfolk make soft noises of surprise. So many people. Their faces bear a hauntedness, a hollow look that puts me in mind of Civil War–era photographs. Only suffering etches a face this way.

They're starving too. We should have brought them food.

We come to a stop outside the hotel, and now I'm expected to do something. Think, Vicki. What do I say? Take me to your leader? Refugees: that is what these people are. They're not likely to have an organized hierarchy.

Tom and Breeze unload the jerry cans and place them on the walkway.

"I wonder," I begin softly. My voice echoes faintly between the buildings. "I wonder if a few of you would sit down with us and talk."

They continue to stare at me in silence. If I wait for them to make the next move, I might not like what it will turn out to be. I look around for a place for us to sit.

Then a little girl breaks from between the ring of adults and comes toward me. Her matted hair sticks out in all directions. She's clad in overalls a few sizes too big for her. She reaches for my hand.

All at once, I know whose hand I'm taking. She's the one who returned Gertie to me.

She guides me down a cracked sidewalk to a spot where the dead grass has been trampled down. In the center stands an empty fire pit, ringed with logs. She takes me inside the circle of logs and presses my hand for me to sit. I do, and I gesture for the townsfolk to do the same.

We wait.

Three of the armed men from the entryway take up positions around us. Not good. Then three women and two men step into the circle and take a seat on the logs across from us. A grizzled woman with a faded yellow bandana takes the seat in the center; the others arrange themselves around her. I've seen this person before. The woman in the darkness, toting water with Alaric. The woman with the shotgun, watching me and Susan from the tree line.

"I'm Vicki," I begin.

"We know who you are," says the woman. Her upper lip keeps disappearing behind her lower one. Only people without teeth can manage this trick.

"And what's your name?"

"That ain't none of your concern."

If I make a misstep here, I've got to find a way to recover, quick.

"We understand," I begin again, "that you're in need of water. And food. We have a small amount of both, but it's not enough for us and…for everyone here."

All their eyes are on me. I look into the ring of faces, seeking out clues. Who are they? Where did they come from? A few have dark skin, but most bear the pale, blue-eyed Northern European features most common to rural West Virginia. I can't work out what gives me this impression, but I don't think they've come from big cities to the east. Maybe they're just local folks whose communities fell apart when their water stopped flowing. Then they followed the faint smudge of green that, until a month ago, still colored the flanks of Cooper's Mountain.

"Gal," the toothless woman drawls, "you're a fool for coming in here. There's some here fixing to drive you off'n your land right now. One or two who'd like to kill you for it."

The townsfolk next to me shuffle uncomfortably. We left behind everything that these people might think of as a weapon.

This whole thing is already starting to go off the rails. I close my eyes and take a deep breath.

I try again. "I need to tell you a few things. The man who was bringing you water, his spring is tapped out. And we think it's because a new outlet opened up, further down the mountain, on my land. My spring's not as good as his was. And it's not enough for all of us. But there is one other source on this mountain, and it's the best one."

"You ain't telling us anything we don't already know."

"So, I...we...the town, we filed a petition for eminent domain..."

The woman sighs and makes as if to rise from her seat.

"We tried to get the courts to make him give us his water—"

"Us? You mean you."

"All of us. Anyone who needed it."

Chortles of disbelief roll through the crowd of onlookers. A man standing next to me, cradling a rifle, mutters a stream of curses under his breath.

"But the court's not responding, so—" They're beginning to shuffle restlessly. I speak louder. "So, here's what I propose. We band together. We go up there to Mr. McMaster's land. And we demand he share his well. With all of us."

"And what if he don't feel up to sharing?"

"You and us together, we're almost a hundred people. He'd be an idiot to say no."

The woman gums her upper lip. She leans back and exchanges a few words I can't hear with the people standing near her.

She turns back to me, frowns, and says, "Go on out of here now. We'll give it a think-over. We'll let you know tomorrow. Go on."

She rises and leaves the circle. The group parts to make way for us. We march solemnly out of Kelso Springs, soldiers on the eve of battle.

Gertie's happiest when she has a job to do. She's set herself a morning schedule around camp. When the sun breaks over the top of the eastern ridge, she rises from sleep and lifts her head to watch the light creep down the trunks of the trees. When it reaches the ground, that's her signal to make sure I'm properly awake.

She searches for places to poke that cold wet nose. If I've left a leg exposed, she'll nudge me right behind the back of my knee. This sends me shooting out from under my blankets, squealing.

Then she pads her way up to the spring. Someone set down a steel water bowl for her a while ago, and we all make sure it stays filled. She starts her day with pure, cold spring water straight out of the black heart of the mountain.

My dog gets more fresh water than any of the humans below in the Springs.

After her morning drink, she and her cold, wet nose make the rounds from one tent to the other. She nudges her way inside; seconds later comes a giggling shriek. If they haven't left the entrance unzipped, she'll yodel to the occupants. I can't call the sound she makes a bark. It's a deep-throated exclamation that, if a human did it, would sound like they'd just said, "Yo!" Sometimes she curls up the end of it like a question: "Yo?"

She'll stand patiently, repeating her call, until they start grousing, "Okay, Gertie. Jeez. We're up." Then she moves on to her next victim.

God forbid anybody's fallen asleep in their camp chair. Any exposed flesh—a dangling hand, a naked foot—is in danger of getting slimed by her slobbery tongue.

Gertie's halfway through her morning rounds when she shouts a warning that someone's approaching the fence.

I recognize two of the men who were guarding the entry to the Springs yesterday. This morning, they're unarmed. They shuffle uneasily, waiting to be acknowledged. Tom and I walk over to them. Neither of us seems to feel the slightest inclination to invite them inside the fence.

The dark-haired man who speaks might be less than thirty years old, but his eyes have already begun to retreat into their sockets. His movements are tightly wound, like a hunting predator's.

He says, "We're in. But we want all of y'all to go with us."

Tom asks, "When?"

"Today." The man gestures at the daylight falling around him. "Noon."

"No weapons," I interject quickly. "None of us armed."

"Then no deal," the man grunts. "If we can't defend ourselves, if we can't press our point, then what are we doing this for?"

"Is there no way we can do this peacefully? Can't we at least try?"

"That ship already done sailed, young lady." The two men turn away from the fence and trudge back down the hill toward Kelso Springs.

Gertie doesn't understand why I'm locking her in the cabin.

Even if I spoke canine, I probably couldn't explain it. I can't claim intuition, not with my track record in life so far, but the prickling just under my skin seems like a warning. Trouble's in the wind, we might have said once, although nowadays there's no wind. Or it's in the mail. But there's no more mail. Maybe it's just my mountain-sense growing in.

I take the trail up to Steen's property and buzz the intercom at his gate.

"Vicki, the way you keep finding excuses to cross my path, I'm beginning to think you're sweet on me."

"Steen, there's people on their way up the mountain right now. They're desperate. You need to make some kind of a deal with them."

"Desperate people don't make deals. They make threats. I don't respond to threats."

"Steen, listen. These people won't hesitate to hurt somebody. These are the same folks who beat Alaric halfway to death."

"Then why'd they spare you guys? You're closer to their camp."

I can hear them approaching: footsteps rustling the leaves as they pick their way up the mountain. Dirt bikes whining up the trail.

"Steen, they're coming. And they're armed."

"You think I'm not? No, Vicki, you really need to stop worrying about me and start looking after yourself. My place is a fortress. Your spring is low-hanging fruit. When they realize how hard it is to get to my source, and how easy it is to get to yours, they'll turn on you."

The security camera pivots and I follow its robotic gaze to the top of Steen's drive, where the first of the people from the Springs have begun to appear.

"You'd better go now, Vicki. Good luck."

Going to the waters, Alaric called it. If he were here, that's how he'd explain what the people from the Springs are doing.

They gather outside Steen's gate. They're heavily armed, as promised. If guns were water, nobody in America would be thirsting.

A few of them narrow their eyes at me when they see me standing at Steen's intercom. Fraternizing with the enemy.

The folks from my water camp arrive next, along with many others from Cooper's Forge. They're armed as well, with hunting rifles and shotguns. Tools for killing groundhogs and deer, not people. I had hoped they would leave their weapons at home. I still hate guns.

"You folks are on private property," Steen's voice buzzes from the intercom, fruity and cheerful. "Police have been called. You need to disperse now."

Early nudges the younger folk aside and approaches the gate. He holds up a stack of legal-sized papers to the black eye of the security camera. He presses the intercom button with a calloused thumb and says, "Young fella, this here is the deed to my farm. A hunnert and twenty acres of pasture, two cow sheds, a hay-baler, and a six-bedroom farmhouse. It's your 'un if you just let these folks have enough water to live."

We wait for Steen's reply. The intercom speaker remains silent. Lights are going off inside the house.

Cool Breeze arrives on his ATV with Rennie. Breeze hops off his machine, swinging a long metal thing I take at first for a rifle. Breeze with a weapon just doesn't compute. Then he swings the object out in front of him: bolt cutters.

He picks a section of fence near the gate and uses the jaws of the cutters to chew into it. Rennie's brought a hacksaw. He takes up a post alongside Breeze and soon they're putting a hurt on that part of the fence.

Steen's front door opens and the muzzle of a rifle pokes out. Behind him, through the sliver of open door, I think I can make out Bill and Newt in the shadows. The two turncoats, or, as some in Cooper's Forge call them, the Judas Brothers.

"Them boys ain't going to shoot their own kin," says Tom.

Breeze and Rennie have managed to cut a jagged gash in the fence, enough for a skinny person to slip through. Rennie sticks his head into it. Breeze pulls him back, but not before the barrel of Steen's gun swings Rennie's way.

Rennie leans into the hole again and says, "Come on, bro. A drink of water's all we want."

Sounds of scuffling reach us from inside the door. The barrel of the rifle bobs around. Then it goes off. Rennie tumbles headfirst through the fence hole, hits his head on Steen's cement drive, and lies still. Blood pools around him.

Every one of us, townsperson and refugee, freezes. That moment, that vision of the dead boy on the driveway, etches itself into our memories. Then silently, solemnly, the people at the front of the mob take out hacksaws and bolt cutters and begin tearing open the fence.

The front door swings open again. Out come Bill and Newt, their hands behind their heads. Their eyes are red and wide. They walk slowly toward the gate.

Someone cocks a gun.

"Sweet Jesus, let 'em through," someone else says softly.

While our eyes are on the twins, Steen breaks cover and sprints across the yard. Some of the Springs people squeeze off a few shots. He makes it to his garage and stumbles inside.

Bill and Newt are instantly forgotten.

We startle at a sudden chugging sound at our feet. The electric motor that opens the gate has started. The gate begins to shudder open. The folks from the Springs fill the widening gap with their bodies, forcing it further apart.

From inside the garage, we hear the revving of an engine. The garage door begins to rise. The folks with guns pepper the opening with bullets.

Before the door is more than partway up, Steen revs the engine and the Lamborghini leaps out of the garage, shattering the half-risen door, heading for the gate.

The men from Kelso Springs who are halfway through the opening realize too late what's about to happen. They writhe and kick against the gate, and against one another. Steen's car smashes into the gate, torquing it to one side. The gate rails give out a horrendous metallic squeal. Then the entire thing crumples around the Lamborghini like a stiff fishing net.

The driver's side door flails open and Steen stumbles, bent double, back toward his garage, half a dozen of the men from the Springs on his heels. A moment later, his quad bolts out of the doorway with three or four huge guys hanging on to it, doing their best to unseat him. He shakes them off and guns it. As he flashes past me, I glimpse his face, wide-eyed, like an animal.

He's off, down the gravel drive. Some of the people on dirt bikes and ATVs chase after him. Many more charge through the open gate, heading toward the well house.

The crowd whoops its victory. A few shots are fired into the air. Some people roll full plastic water barrels out of the storage shed; others are guzzling it on the spot and dousing each other in mock-Baptisms. Most of the Cooper's Forge brigade still stands outside the gate, staring in at the debauchery. These people, dying from lack of water this morning, are now drunk on it, savagely prancing around in blood-stained puddles.

Rennie, Newt, and four men from the Springs whose names I never knew, they won't be needing any more water.

❧

No police come. No help arrives from anywhere. We bring the bodies down from the mountain on the backs of ATVs, lay them on folding tables in the church basement, and cover them with white linen tablecloths. None of us can think of what to do with them next.

So, we do what everyone in Cooper's Forge does in times of distress. We head to Althea's.

We sit around her living room on Afghan-draped couches and wing-back chairs, sipping black coffee, our heads hanging low. Althea rests her chin on her cane, eyes closed. Praying, maybe. Susan makes her way to the kitchen and comes back with Althea's bottle of bourbon. We pass it around. I accept a healthy splash of it in my coffee.

"Who's going to tell Rennie's mama?"

"I'll do it." Lila sips her coffee. "They've known me longest."

"And Newt?"

"Give him to his brother," says Happ.

"Let one damned traitor bury another," Early growls. "He ain't none of our concern."

Althea breaks in with a voice like thunder. "Now, y'all can stop that right there. You're in my house and I ain't having it. Them's Cooper's Forge boys, and you with your noses in the air don't change that none." She sniffs loudly and returns to her kitchen.

"Reckon we'll do both funerals on the same day."

"What about them four from the Springs? We don't even know their names or where their kin are at."

Althea passes around little China plates and silver dessert forks. At the center of each plate, a curl of nutmeg-scented steam rises from a square of something blackish brown. I probe at it with my fork. Cakey, but moist, verging on custard. I take a taste, and I melt.

"Althea, this is so good. What is it?"

"Persimmon pudding."

I help myself to seconds, and then thirds. Somewhere between the pudding, the bourbon, the raw wound of the violence that took place before my eyes, and the relief of knowing that the Kelso Springs folks now have all the water they need, I come undone. It's as if all the springs inside me have burst open. I excuse myself, step into Althea's bathroom, and sob into a towel. I clean myself up, return to the couch, pour another dollop of bourbon into my cup, take a long swig, and fall asleep.

The next thing I know, the sun is up and Althea, in a long pink house dress, is shaking my shoulder. "Get up, now, honey."

Tom, Early, Susan, and Breeze are standing in the middle of Althea's living room.

"Something's happened. Up at Steen's."

"What?" I take in their funereal expressions. "Tom, what happened?"

"The well pump's broke."

"Broke?"

"They let it run all night. It was a variable speed pump; wasn't meant to run like that. They left the pressure on too high. The pump blew out, busted a pipe, and the whole thing silted in."

"Silted in?"

"It filled up with sand."

"The well's got to be cleared out," Susan explains. "The pump needs replaced. No more water coming out of that well for a while, I reckon."

"Call the county," I offer hopefully. "They'll send someone."

Tom shakes his head. "Tried. Nobody available for a site this remote. That's what they said. Apparently, they got bigger fish to fry."

"That's crazy. People are dying up here."

"What do we do now?" Susan whispers.

I glance around the room. Their eyes are on me. Vicki Truax from Delaney Street now has the only source of water for miles around.

I say softly, "We'd best be getting back to the spring."

10

We pile into Tom's faded blue truck, but instead of turning left and starting the bumpy climb up the mountain, he stays on the road for another half mile, and turns off onto a derelict gravel path I've never noticed before.

"Tom? What's the plan here? Aren't we going up to the spring?"

"Got a stop to make first."

He pulls into a yard full of rusted cars. Hundreds of them. Small leafless trees grow through the bodies of some. Their headlights, smashed, glassless and hollow, remind me of the eyes of people in old folks' homes, hopeless and unseeing.

Carl is here, and some of the others, working with crowbars, prying off hoods and doors and loading them into truck beds. The folks tumble out of Tom's truck and begin to do the same.

I stand in the middle of the commotion, dumb and disbelieving.

We join a cavalcade of loaded trucks and ATV wagons heading up to the spring. Some have brought car parts, others have bags of cement or sand, straw bales, cinderblocks.

Gertie bounds up, nuzzles my knees, and weaves herself in and out of my legs. I bend down and kiss her knobby dome of a head, then I survey the scene before me.

I've never seen so many people here before. Some are stacking their cargo around the outside of the fence, fortifying it. That makes sense. The simple chain link made to stop itinerant baseballs at Little League games can be breached with a good pair of bolt cutters.

Other folks are pulling car parts and cinderblocks inside the fence. A few of Cooper's Forge's burliest men work with chain saws to cut the fallen trees into stout sections of log. They drag the logs inside the fence and stand them upright, forming a wall around the spring itself. The inner keep of a makeshift castle.

On the rocks atop the spring, someone has built a slapdash shed with slits at the top. A guardhouse. Anyone standing in it would be able to see people approaching long before they got close. A chill runs through my stomach. The slits are for rifles.

Then I realize just how many of the people here are armed. Rifles slung across backs. Pistols in leather holsters. Shotguns resting up against rocks. I hate guns. I hate guns.

I wonder in disbelief at what my peaceful mountain home has become. Then it hits me, hard as a punch to the gut.

It's *not* mine anymore.

I lose track of time, wandering among the chaos. I might be weeping. I can't feel my face, or my feet.

Dim and far-off, I hear someone say, "Somebody go take care of Vicki."

A quilt goes around my shoulders. A hand takes mine and squeezes, gently. From what seems like far away, Cool Breeze says, "Come on, Vicki Truax, we got a seat for you." Breeze steers me by the shoulders to a camp chair close to the stove. He presses a tin cup into my hands. The hot coffee inside it warms my palms.

Rennie lost his life yesterday, I say silently to myself. It doesn't seem real. I distract myself by placing his death in the abstract. What Rennie lost is a thing I can't define, yet I'm nothing without it. It's the one great mystery we all dance around: precious, yet unknowable. And so horribly fragile. A gift, revocable at any second, never to be given back.

My mind drifts idly like this for a while, but then it lands on the impossibility of the situation we're facing. What will happen to us if the Kelso Springs folks manage to get inside our barrier? What will happen to them if our fortifications work?

To this question, I think I know the answer. The elderly will die first. The frail and the ill. Then the children. After a while, the adults will sicken, and they too will begin to die. It's already begun.

Darkness wells up like ink from the valley below. The sun sinks away in a cloudless glow of orange-to-lavender-to-teal. Tom ambles up and takes a seat beside me. "I understand how you feel, Miss Vicki."

"No, you don't, Tom."

"You got a tender heart. It's why we all love you. But sooner or later, them folks down there, they're going to pay us the same wage they paid Steen."

Nobody's told me anything about Steen's fate. Whether the boys on their dirt bikes caught up to him. I decide then and there I don't want to know.

"So, you think, if the tables were turned, if they were holding this spring and we were the ones down there, dying of thirst—"

"Then we'd be the ones getting ready to attack."

"That's it, then? No alternatives? Just violence?"

"Come on, Vicki. You know well as any of us, there ain't enough for everyone. We share with them, we just prolong their agony, and we sentence ourselves to death along with them. Don't you think some of us ought to live?"

Tom's face is turned toward me in the dim light. He doesn't do rhetorical questions. He really is waiting for an answer.

"I just...can't accept that there's no solution...where we all get to live."

"And what d'you expect we should do in the meantime? Vicki, I know this is your property and all, but—"

"Tom, you and I both know that doesn't mean a thing anymore."

"All right. But think of it this way: wouldn't none of us still be alive if the people of this town hadn't excavated that spring. Don't that count for something?"

"But, Tom, the people wouldn't have had a spring to excavate if those two boys from the Springs hadn't blasted out the rock."

"Illegally, Vicki. Illegally."

My head is pounding. "I think we just went in a circle there."

❧

Who makes the ultimate decision, who lives and who dies? Whose water is it?

I don't sleep. Not in any meaningful sense. You can't call the monotonous sadism I'm performing on myself "sleep." I'm aware through the night that the people of the town have set up watches. At any time, I can count at least six people, crouched behind their castle wall of car parts and leftover home projects, pointing the business-end of a gun out into the darkness beyond the chain-link fence. They take it in shifts, one group relieving the other every few hours. I'm sure some are keeping watch up in the turret above the spring too.

These same thoughts spin through my mind, over and over. I'm on a ghastly merry-go-round ride that doesn't end, me and all the people of this town, on the bony backs of desiccated zombie-animals, galloping, gape-mouthed, around and around the same dried-up cluster of skeletal trees. Many times, I wake up in the middle of the night, playing these same thoughts through to where the end loops back to the beginning.

I haven't admitted, even to myself, how much I miss Alaric's calm, parsimonious wisdom. The eye of every storm. He'd find a way to meet justice head-on.

WWAD: What Would Alaric Do?

Toward daybreak, I become conscious of something warm on my lap. As the darkness thins, I make out Gertie's head resting on my knees. She's looking up at me, expectantly.

I hook up the coil, gather up as many enamel coffee cups as I can find, and fill them from the reservoir basin. I set them on the coil. Gertie and I make the rounds. She provides the cold nose to rouse them from slumber. I go around whispering, "Hey, when you're up, come get some coffee. We need to talk."

When almost everybody's joined me, I stand to speak. All eyes are on me. What did I do to command this much attention from them? Some know-nothing city girl who showed up out of the blue, why do they even bother with me?

"Look. I know we're in a tough spot here," I begin. They're waiting, nodding. Go on, girl. "I just don't think I can live with letting the people down in the valley go without water. I know, I know, there's not enough to go around. But maybe, instead of cutting them off, we should cut back to bare minimum ourselves."

All around the circle of chairs, I see mouths turning down, brows furrowing. But I charge ahead. "Half a gallon for each of us, including them. It's not enough in the long term, but maybe if we buy some time, for all of us, something will turn up, and they won't have to die. And we don't have to worry about getting shot."

They blink at me in silence. They toe the gravel beneath their chairs. Shuffle uncomfortably.

Then Susan speaks. "You know, Vicki, you got a car. You got friends outside Cooper's Forge. Maybe you ought to give some thought to getting out while you can."

"What? You're just going to get rid of me?"

"No, no, honey, we're just looking out for you. You got someplace to go; we don't. This is our home, always has been. We got no choice but to defend it."

"Or you could share it."

"We share it, we're all as good as dead. You know that."

"Maybe, maybe not. But at least we won't go out of this life as complete assholes."

"Watch your mouth, young lady, they's Christians here."

"Can't we at least put it to a vote?"

"Sit down, Vicki."

What else can I do? I sit down hard, my cheeks flushing hot.

The morning routine starts up around camp. Biscuits baking, wall-mending. The townsfolk make a show of forgiving me for my blasphemy. They pour extra honey on my biscuit, keep my coffee cup topped, squeeze my shoulder as they walk behind my chair. Carl lays a blackish-brown strip of something on my knee. At first, I think this must be a treat for Gertie. But he says, "Deer jerky. It's a little stiff; soak it in your coffee for a bit. Been a couple years since I shot that one. But I reckon it's still all right."

They make a point of not leaving me on my own. They sit in threes and fours. I can tell they're making an effort to keep the conversation going.

"I'm old enough to remember when they first started saying on the news that wars of the future was going to be folks fighting over water," says Carl.

"Water wars."

"We all thought it'd happen somewhere else. I-raq. Bot-see-wana. One of them places. Not here in the U S of A."

That's what we all think. It would happen to *their* water. Never to *our* water. I drift back to that summer evening at Alaric's cabin. Alaric dribbling water from a cup into the palm of his hand, trying to help me make the leap of mind from "my water" to "the water."

I sense it's time for me to chip into the conversation, so I say, "When I was a kid, my mom would take me to the Baltimore County Fair. There was a game on the midway called Water Wars. You'd pay three dollars to shoot water balloons out of a slingshot, try to soak your friends."

"Now we shoot *bullets* at our friends, and we try to *keep* from soaking them," Susan adds, absently.

"Them folks ain't our friends."

"If circumstances were different, maybe they would be."

"If circumstances were different, but they ain't," says Carl. "Last winter I went up the creek to see if I could find any more deer. I found this feller in the stream bed. Hunter like me. His canteen had run out. Skin all puckered up. Mice had ate his eyeballs. I ain't going out like that. I don't hold nothing personal against those folks in the Springs. But I'm going to live, Vicki. I want to live."

"Yeah," I say, and it comes out sounding petulant. "So do they."

❧

Rainless December gives way to snowless January. Despite the tension all around us, we still drift into idle moments at camp.

The talk dwindles into silence, the trees stand utterly still, and I close my eyes and slide slowly backward in time, deeper and deeper in, as though I'm descending into a well.

Before the townsfolk pitched in to excavate, we had no more than a trickle here.

Before the trickle, a pair of moonshiners worked out the best site to dynamite for water. Without their action, we'd have nothing.

Before them, this spring was buried under land inherited by an anchorless girl from Delaney Street, who would never have known to look for water on it.

Before that, it was the home of a mountain woman, heart of gold and nerves of granite, who made much out of little. But that was in a time when no one had to think about water.

Before her, generations of mountaineers, coopers, and miners drank from the heart of this mountain, their haunted faces long since faded from the daguerreotype of history.

Before them, the deep-time dwellers of this mountain, who revered as sacred that which we can't stop thinking of as a right, who saw any water as every water, to whom disrespecting the waters counted as the gravest of sins.

Before them, there were no humans in this place at all. No creatures who could rise above their moment-to-moment quest to survive. They could know only what water *is*, but never what water *means*.

I do think seriously about leaving. Without me here, it would free up an extra half-gallon a day for someone else. But it would also mean abdicating every bit of control I have over this nightmare. If I stay, I might be able to shift the situation.

Susan comes to sit by me. Whenever I'm in anguish, torturing myself mentally with one thing or another, she appears. Friends, I've had throughout my life. But I've never had Susan, who understands me better when I don't speak a word than other people do when I say a bucketful.

She hands me a beer, a wanton luxury since alcohol dehydrates. "Penny for your thoughts?"

"I'm just remembering this awful thought experiment they made us do in philosophy class," I tell her. "The nukes are about to drop. You're the leader of a group of twenty people, you have the keys to a fallout shelter that will keep people alive until the danger is over, but there's only room for ten."

"Oh God. We got that one in eleventh grade with Miss Lewellyn. I hated it! Why do they even do that?"

"Not sure. But sometimes I think real life puts people in that kind of situation. You remember a few years back, on the news, all those kids showing up on the southern border, all by themselves? More little young souls than anyone was prepared for, and more kept coming every day?"

She sips her beer. "Honey, we don't get much of that kind of news out here."

"Everyone was talking about the only two choices, both awful. Let them all in and overrun the resources of the people on the border. Or turn them away, back to violence and starvation."

The memory swallows me for a moment. Susan waits a beat. Then she prompts, "Go on."

"At the time, I thought, holy shit, this is just like that godawful thought experiment. And my answer to the situation at the border, with those kids—it was the same as my answer to the fallout shelter thing."

"Me, I just refused to do the damned thing. Got an F. My folks were pee-oh'd."

"But if you refuse to make a choice, in the scenario, everyone dies."

"Well, what, then? Which one did you pick?"

"Thing is, even the way the scenario is presented to you, it's making you think there are only two choices. Plan A: put everyone in the shelter and, most likely, all twenty of them die. Or Plan B: pick the ten people who least deserve to live and toss them out. They even give you profiles on all the people so you can debate who's most worthy of a spot in the shelter."

"But Vicki Truax, she don't play by everyone else's rules." Susan laughs.

"See, the whole experiment is artificial because it's assuming a fixed set of variables. But if it were a real-life situation, like those kids at the border, or like this whole thing about the water, there's hundreds of possibilities. There's not just Plan A and Plan B. There's an unknown number of things that could make up Plan C. And somewhere among them, there's gotta be a course of action that lets everyone live."

"Well, shit, then let's go all in on Plan C!"

"In this case, we find a way forward that doesn't sacrifice one life for another. Or we die trying. As long as we're alive, we never give up on anyone."

She blows out a long breath, leans into her chair, and tilts her face toward the stars. Then she asks the question for which I have no answer: "Okay, then. So, what's our Plan C?"

In the morning, I wake up with an idea fully formed. I wait until the folks around camp are occupied with something else. Then I make my way to the reservoir.

I lift the wooden lid, plunge in a plastic milk jug, and draw it out about a quarter full. I fill my steel thermos bottle to the brim and screw on the cap. I take two cans of peaches from the makeshift larder we built beside the reservoir and stuff them into my pack. They were *my* peaches anyway, some of the last of what came with me from my apartment in Baltimore.

I try my best to slip through the gap in the fence unseen. Susan's rolling out a spool of barbed wire along an outside section of the fence, and she spots me before I can get far.

"Hey, Miss Vicki, what're you up to?"

"Look," I say quietly, hoping not to attract attention. "This is half my water ration for the day. I'm going to give it to one of the kids down at the Springs."

"Are you out of your mind?"

"Listen. What somebody my size needs in a day—that would

do for two of those little ones. I drink half; one kid drinks all they need. See? I'm healthy and I'm a grown-up. I can get by on half."

"No, you can't. Vicki, that's suicide."

"I'll be okay, for a while anyway. In time, who knows what could happen. It might save somebody. It might make a difference. At least it's better than waiting around like this until people start killing each other."

She studies me, wide-eyed. A kaleidoscope of emotion tumbles across her face. Then her expression softens. "You're the bravest person I ever met." She squeezes my shoulder. "Count me in. That's two we'll save today."

Susan fills up a second thermos bottle and makes her way to join me outside the fence without anyone noticing her. We set off downhill toward Kelso Springs.

"Did you want to tell somebody what we're up to?"

I smile. "This is Cooper's Forge, hon. We don't have to say a word and it'll still be all over town in an hour."

She chuckles. "You know us pretty good."

As we draw closer, we both fall silent. We crouch inside a tangle of overgrown forsythia vine. We're close enough to see a stretch of the gravel road leading to the Springs. Nobody's in sight, but the prickling hairs along the back of my neck give me reason to believe the place is as heavily guarded as ever.

Susan and I look at each other. Now what?

Somewhere ahead, the tall grass begins to rustle. Three little girls pop out onto bare ground beside the road. They look furtively over their shoulders, toward the Springs. When they're satisfied they've evaded the guards, they plop down into the dust and begin a make-believe game with plastic horses.

My stomach pitches, seeing how thin they are. They're so grubby I can't make out their features. But if they're well enough to play, that's reason enough to hope.

I take out our two bottles and slowly ease them out in front of me.

"Psst!" The girls look up, startled. I wave and point to the bottles. "For you!"

I pat Susan's shoulder and motion for us start back up the trail. If we stick around, the girls might suspect we want something for it.

The three come running over at once. The oldest passes the bottles to the two youngest first. When they've had their fill, she drinks. Then she calls out to us. "Thank you, dog lady."

I turn and grin at her. "Gertie says hi."

Susan says, "We'll be back with some more tomorrow. Can you meet us here? Just you three?"

The tallest girl scratches her scalp with two long fingers and rubs the back of her left leg with the toes of her right. She sways back and forth, considering me. "You got any food?"

I remember the two cans of peaches I stuffed in my pack. I take them out and roll them downhill to the kids. They grab the food and dash away.

"Well, Miss Vicki, for better or worse, we done it now," Susan says with a heavy sigh. "Their parents are going to want to know where they got all that."

When we get back to camp, Early growls, "Where you two been?" No one else seems to have noticed our disappearance.

For the rest of the afternoon, I keep busy, stirring a pot of ham beans warming on the coil for the camp's supper. It's quiet work that won't make me thirsty. I catch Susan's eye once or twice, but we both look away quickly. I'm beginning to think we can get away with this.

It's hypnotic, pot-stirring in the dusty evening sunshine. I start to doze off. I half-notice when Carl goes over to the fence and speaks to someone on the other side. Then he turns and marches straight toward me, his bottom lip poking out. I'm suddenly wide awake.

"Little girl out there wants to talk to the dog lady." He jabs a thumb over his shoulder.

Early looks over at me sharply. "Girl, what in hell did you do?"

All eyes are on me as I cross the compound to the place where Carl was talking. The tallest of the three girls stands there, bare-footed.

She sees me but doesn't smile. She says, "My mama said Tyrell's going to Jesus tonight if he don't get something to eat. So, I give him my peaches."

I kneel so I'm eye-level with her, across a mesa of cinder-block and barbed wire. I press my face to the chain link.

"Tyrell. Is that your brother?"

She nods.

"I'm Vicki."

She nods again.

"What's your name?"

"Daddy says not to tell."

"When's the last time you ate something?"

"I ain't ate since Sunday."

"Wait right there."

I return to the kettle of ham beans and I ladle my tin cup full of them. I carry the cup toward the gap in the compound fence that serves us as a gate.

"What in hell—" Early begins.

I show him my hand.

I carry the cup of beans outside the gate and hand it to the girl. As I'm turning to go back, Susan comes up behind me with her own cup of beans and hands it to the girl.

"Give this one to your brother, honey, and tell him we all hope he feels better."

What happens next charms me to pieces. Along comes Carl with a plastic bag full of dried apple rings. "You tuck that in your pocket, now, young lady." He turns away gruffly and lopes back inside the compound.

Susan and I exchange glances. We head back inside to face the inquisition.

The townsfolk form a ring around us. I try to read their

expressions. Some are outright angry; others, I can't be sure.

"You three," Early fumes, "you had no right. That was our food you done give away."

"It was my food." I match his tone. I've never spoken to any of them like this. "It was my portion, and I'm choosing to give it to her."

"Same with me," Susan proclaims. We both look over at Carl.

"I grew them apples two summers ago. It's my say-so, who gets to eat 'em."

"You know what happens next? They're all going to be up here, hanging off that fence, begging for a hand-out. And the minute we don't give it to 'em, what do you think their parents are going to do?"

"It was fixing to happen sooner or later, Early," says Lila. "Them three just cut short the waiting, is all."

As evening deepens, the camp dogs bark a warning. Carl runs a flashlight beam across the perimeter and lights up three small figures. The girls from the road are sitting cross-legged in the leaves, just outside the fence. They're not alone. Our flashlight beams pick up at least half a dozen more children, huddled here and there under bushes, sharing blankets.

The adults arrive later that night. A few drape tarps over saplings and stake them down to form pup tents against the night chill. One young guy with a pointy black beard and a white Natty Boh cap pulls up a log and sits at the edge of the fence, studying us. That familiar one-eyed cartoon figure, the symbol of Baltimore's home-town beer, stands out like a beacon in a West Virginia woods. I wonder what connects him to my former city. I'm not planning on walking up and starting a conversation, though. There's something in his gaze that makes the hairs on my arms prickle.

By daybreak, our camp inside the chain-link fence is half-rimmed with another camp. The children talk quietly among themselves and devise games with twigs and pebbles.

The adults sit and watch us. Their eyes follow our every move.

11

I'm not the least bit hungry, yet. But my head is pounding, and my kidneys ache. The back of my throat burns like somebody rubbed it with an emery board.

I had tried to pace myself, to make my half-ration last all day, but by the time the sun climbed to the tops of the tallest poplars, I had finished it off.

Alaric once told me that when native people went on long journeys, they would hold a pebble in their mouths to stave off thirst. I wipe off a pebble and place it between my cheek and gum. It works, for about an hour.

I tell myself to woman up. I tell myself it's only until tomorrow, then I'll get another quart. For some reason, that makes it worse.

Breeze sidles over at one point and says out of the corner of his mouth, "Here you go, Vicki Truax, you take a swig off my canteen."

I drink. My head clears a little.

It's almost midnight. The last water I had was a few furtive sips from Breeze's canteen, hours ago. But in minutes, a new day starts. I can take my next half-ration.

I've been counting the seconds, lashing my feverish tongue around inside my mouth, because if I let it sit in one place too long, it sticks to my gums.

My own watch hasn't worked in months, so I've borrowed Susan's. By the time the last few minutes tick down, I'm standing over the reservoir with my jug in hand.

At ten seconds past midnight, I scoop my ration and begin gulping it down. My stomach lurches. The water I've waited so long for comes spewing back up, spattering the dusty ground.

Note to self: small sips, Vicki, small sips.

In the end, I have to hide my water from myself to avoid the temptation to gulp it down until it's gone. I set my jug at the back of my tent and cover it with a sleeping bag. It's still burning a hole in my mind. The one thing that keeps me from rushing into the tent and devouring it is the knowledge that the folks on the other side of the fence have gone without water for much longer than I have.

At first, it's just me, and Susan, and Tom on half rations. Then Cool Breeze renounces half his ration. Early won't speak to any of the four of us. Whenever he passes near us, he levels us with his most withering stink-eye.

Once a day, a cavalcade of pickup trucks take water down the mountain to the few folks remaining back in town. They go heavily armed.

It's getting harder to pass half our rations to the folks outside the fence. We try handing our water to the children directly, but twice now, adults have shoved their way in and grabbed the cups right out of the children's hands.

Yesterday, in the middle of all the shoving, the water spilled onto the rocky forest floor. For the rest of my life, I'll be trying to forget the sight of women and men licking the wet rocks, damming the dripping water with cupped hands, sucking the last bit of moisture from their fingers.

We take it in turns to walk around the inside of the fence, looking for places where someone's bent up the chain link, or broken through the links themselves, or tried to dig beneath. We hardly ever catch them at it, but we always find evidence of someone trying to get in.

One of the men outside the compound has taken to shooting through the fence at random objects in our camp. A coffee pot. A camp chair. Each time he shoots, he chooses a target closer to a person. Then one of his bullets buries itself in the hind leg of Lila's Beagle, Scooter. The dog leaps into the air with an ear-splitting squeal, and races around the inside of the fence, dragging his bleeding leg and yelping loudly enough to make the trees ring. Susan catches Scooter and holds him tight while Carl digs the bullet out of his leg, then pulls off his own boot and wraps the wound with a gray woolen sock. Scooter keeps up his anguished yowling all through the night.

The people from the Springs call out to us. They beg for a chance to live. They taunt us. They call us monsters. The townsfolk hurl their insults right back at them.

It's starting to come apart.

⮞

My dried-out mind doesn't work as well as it did when it had enough water. I can't seem to wrap my head around a way to end this standoff without people dying. My poor little shriveled raisin-brain can't connect the dots.

I keep thinking the same thought, over and over. It isn't even a complete thought. Just an action, floating in nothing, without another action to follow it. But I figure, the longer I wait, the harder it will be to do anything.

I stay awake through the night, chewing a quid of sassafras leaves. I've long since sucked the last of the moisture from them, but their faintly root-beery flavor keeps my mouth damp.

When it's that completely bloodless time between deep night and early morning, I rise from my sleeping bag, so slowly and quietly that even Gertie doesn't stir. I step carefully around Breeze and Carl, half-dozing in their chairs at the makeshift gate that closes the gap in the fence and serves as our only way in or out. I slip through the gate without making a sound.

I move in shadows, uphill. Not until I'm certain I'm far out of sight and earshot of our compound do I dare to move openly on the path. The night is cool, so unlike those broiling summer days when I first arrived. An anemic sliver of a moon drifts overhead, soaking my woods in a weak and watery light.

The silhouette of my cabin comes into view. My heart leaps into my throat, then falls into my bowels. I know, long before my senses give any evidence, it's been ransacked.

Its door hangs open. My things are gone. Loose bits of

trash are scattered across the floor. Aunt Colleen's bed has been stripped of its comforter and goose-down tick mattress. The rope that once held the smoked ham dangles, a frayed end where someone sawed through it. Every jar is gone from the shelf, dark rings where they once sat collecting dust, as though they left their shadows behind them.

I don't dare click on my flashlight. I step onto the butcher-block table and feel along the ceiling beam, right where it meets the roof. My hand closes around the T-shirt-wrapped bundle. I climb down, tuck it under my hoodie, and make my way silently back to camp.

I have no plan for this bundle of dynamite. I've never known why I kept it. But now my cobwebbed brain is telling me it's important, so here it is, next to my skin.

I nearly make it back to camp undetected. I'm feeling my way along the outer bulwarks, making for the gate, when a figure rises up out of the darkness. He flicks on a pen light near his face. The momentary blast of light illuminates his finger pressed against his lips.

"You're Vicki," he whispers. Not a question.

"I'm armed," I say reflexively, "and I can scream."

"I want you to get me inside your camp. To talk." His voice reminds me of dry leaves.

"I can't help you there. They won't even listen to me." I turn to go.

"My kids. My kids are dying, Vicki."

An hour later, sunrise is in the mail, and the man is sitting on a log inside our compound. I sit beside him, waiting for the rest of the townsfolk to join us. As the darkness thins, I get my first look at him. He's wearing faded jeans and a thick green flannel shirt with leather patches at the elbows. He's got the drawn, unkempt face of a refugee, but in better times, I'd probably guess he's younger than me.

I hand him a half-cup of my water. That means even less for me today.

"You know my name. I don't know yours."

I wait for him to volunteer his name. He doesn't.

Early and the others are plenty mad when they see I've let in an outsider. I offer no resistance; I just wait until their rage subsides and at last, they're sitting down to listen.

The man in the green flannel shirt begins to speak without preamble. "Look, I'm going to propose something that will be good for you and good for me. I got six kids. Over there." He gestures to a spot in the darkness outside the fence. "Only two are mine. The others belong to other families. You take them in, give them just a few sips of water a day. The folks on the outside aren't going to shoot you if there's a risk of hitting their children. You save them. They save you. Deal?"

"A human shield?" Carl wrinkles his nose.

"Call it whatever you want. Just give these kids a chance to live."

Carl chews the end of his beard. Then he says, "Hurry up. Bring 'em in here before it gets too light."

Six kids end up being fourteen. Parents catch on to what we're doing and shove their children forward. Gertie goes around to each child, noses their hands, and nuzzles their knees. A few of the children throw their arms around her rumpled neck and won't let go. Gertie licks their cheeks and patiently endures their squeezing. It takes us a while to get them settled around the camp stove, to find them enough extra blankets, and to pour a few sips of life-saving water and a spoonful of applesauce into each of them.

They're remarkably un-childlike in their docility. It creeps me out, how quiet they are. Dying children: not much inclined to misbehave.

Although daylight is breaking, the kids curl up next to each other and fall asleep, as though this is the first time they've felt safe in ages. Gertie plops down in the middle of the kid pile and glances over at me as if to say, I've found my purpose. So many of them are vying for a spot next to Gertie's furry warmth, I can barely make her out among the tangle of tiny arms and legs.

As the sun rises and the adults in the camp begin to stir, I crawl inside my tent and feel around for the T-shirt-wrapped lump I stowed beneath my sleeping bag. I unwrap it and sit cross-legged on my heap of blankets, holding the bundle of dynamite. I turn it over and over. Six cardboard cylinders circling a seventh, bound by two wraps of electrical tape. Braided fuses extend from one end, gather in a bundle, then come together to form a single, thick fuse as long as my forearm. It's lighter than I would have expected. I raise it to my nose. The scent reminds me of wet cement, with a hint of battery acid.

I still don't know what compelled me to fish it out of my cabin, any more than I've ever known what made me put it there in the first place, let alone covet it all this time. I hate myself for keeping secrets from these people who've never been anything but kind to me. What could I possibly want with this thing?

A phrase I've heard on the news is trying to swim up into my consciousness. It's floating in a shoal of words like *desperation*, *last-ditch*, and *zero-sum*. If that's the company it keeps, I don't want anything to do with it. I shudder and push it back down into the darker waters of my subconscious.

I turn the bundle of cool cardboard cylinders over and over in my hands. The coating on the outside is waxy. This standoff could end in so many ways, but none of them have all of us walking out of here alive. I hold an image in my mind of each of the people of Cooper's Forge who occupy this compound with me. When it comes down to sheer survival, when they're face to face with the end, what will they do?

So, what are my options? I can't threaten to blow up actual people. Most of Cooper's Forge, and a fair number of folks from the Springs, know me well enough to call my bluff.

I could threaten to light it off inside the mouth of the spring, and maybe collapse it, if they don't agree to a truce. Would that even work? Probably not.

But there is one thing that might.

All at once, that elusive phrase I was searching for bobs up and pierces the surface of my mind. It's hideous. It turns my guts to ash. But it's the perfect description for what I must do. To myself. To break this stalemate.

The phrase is *nuclear option*.

12

Someone's tugging at the cuff of my jeans and it isn't Gertie.

The sleep that sneaks up on you is the hardest to wake from. Evening shadows are already creeping up the tree trunks. I've slept the day away, cradling a bundle of explosives.

As I wake, I rummage around for the dynamite and quickly stow it under a pile of clothes. Then I look to see who's pulling at me. It's the copper-haired girl who brought back Gertie.

"Hi, honey," I stammer.

"Will you let my daddy come inside the fence?" she says without preamble. Her words are colorless, bleached dry of emotion. "They're going to start shooting soon. I want him in here with me."

"Sweetie, I can't—"

"He won't drink any of your water. I promise. I just want him with me is all. Don't let him die out there all by himself."

"They're not going to let me bring anybody else in. I'm sorry."

She leaves me without another word. She marches straight for the gate. She steps over the boots of the two Cooper's Forge boys on duty, wraps her twig-like fingers around the chain-link and tries to tug it open. When the people from the Springs see what she's doing, they surge toward the fence.

Tom pulls her away. "Hey, hey, there. What're you doing?"

She offers him no resistance. She says, "Going out to my daddy."

Now, the curly-haired man is on the other side of the fence. He calls to his daughter. Their fingers entwine through the chain link. He says, "Don't come out, honey."

The girl's face crumples but her eyes make no tears. "I want to be with you."

"I'll be right here. I promise. But you got to stay put. Will you do that? For me?"

He pushes his arm through the gap in the chain link so that she can clasp his hand. The moment the gap opens, the people outside the fence become a human tide, surging forward, spreading the gap, pouring into the compound.

The Cooper's Forge folks clamber up to stave them off. They scuffle in the half-dark. Blows land on the backs of desperate people. The twisted sounds coming from their throats don't sound human. God, where are the children in all this?

The moment for my nuclear option has come already. I thought I'd have more time.

I race for my tent and grab the bundle of dynamite from my pile of clothes. I pour camp-stove fuel on my flannel shirt, wrap it around a pair of kitchen tongs, and light it from the coil. I pick a tall patch of rocks, far enough away from the people and the spring, but where I'm plenty visible. I climb to the top, lugging the dynamite and my handmade torch. I stand as tall as I can, holding both aloft.

After a few moments, I have their attention.

"Oh God, honey, no!" Susan's voice rises through the crowd.

"What you think you're gonna to do with that?" a voice yells from the darkness.

Good question. I try to compose my demand. My torch is beginning to sputter. My heart drops into my hiking boots. This is not going to work.

A faint scuttling comes from the rocks behind be. I turn to see who it is, but I'm blinded by my own torch light. Someone knocks into me from behind. I drop the bundle and throw my hands up in front of me to break my fall. I hit the rocks, hard. My vision's lolloping around in my head, but I catch a glimpse of Natty Boh winking at me from the front of a ballcap. He's fumbling around in the dark. He's got the dynamite and now he's off, leaping down the rocks and into the middle of the crowd.

He yells, "All y'all get out! Or I swear to God! I'm lighting it!"

People I can't identify rush in at him. All I can see is a tangle of bodies in the gloom. Then, with a hiss, the faces of the people in the scrum are lit by a sparkle of white-gold light.

"He lit it! Shit! He lit it!"

Someone grabs the dynamite and tosses it on the ground. A whole army of booted feet stomp at the lighted end. The bundle rolls and skitters around in the dust, but the fuse dazzles stubbornly. Someone throws a camp blanket over it. It dims for a moment, then eats neatly through the flannel.

"Aw, shit! Somebody get a knife. Cut the damn thing."

Camp knives and switchblades are tossed to them. But now the one long fuse is spent and the nine short ones have caught.

Then Early Slade leaps up and out of the darkness and grabs the lit bundle off the ground. He tucks it in his coat, slings himself through the gate, and goes hurtling down the trail. He hits the lip of the cliff and keeps on going. When the dynamite explodes, he is in midair, with his body wrapped tightly around it.

৵

We don't speak. We don't look into one another's eyes. We barely lift our feet when we walk. My heart is rigid and cold as a tombstone, as though I'm dying from the inside out. Judging from their faces, I'd say my neighbors are struggling with similar lumps of stone in their own chests.

What Early did drains the fight out of us. For a time. Long enough to usher the outsiders back on their side of the fence. Silence hangs, thick and heavy as an ash cloud.

Susan's sitting with me, and so is Mack. We've been talking a while. We might have a plan.

"So, you think they'll go for it?"

"We can't but try."

Most of the Cooper's Forge folks have spent the better part of the night seated around the burgundy-red glow of the stove coil. Hours ago, somebody passed around cups of coffee, but they've long since gone cold. The scent of dynamite still clings faintly to the night air.

The three of us approach. We stand and wait to be noticed.

When most of the folks have turned their gaze to us, I say quietly, "Evening, all. We gals have got an idea if you'll listen."

The group erupts into grumbles.

Susan begins, "Now look, y'all. What Vicki done tonight gave us a second chance—"

"And got poor old Early killed," Carl grumbles.

"Well, I think we owe her a listen," Susan insists calmly. She gestures to me with her eyes.

"Now, hear us out on this one," I begin. I sound more confident than I am. "Say we call a truce. Make a peace offering. A pint of water for everybody on the other side of the fence."

More grumbling. A few people stand up to leave.

"Hang on, hang on. There's more." Susan waves them back into their seats.

"Benadryl," I tell them, "and vodka." They stare at me blankly. "It's the classic date rape drug. We three are gonna sneak into town and come back with all the vodka and Benadryl we can find."

Most of the townsfolk shake their heads. But I look to Tom, Happ, and a few others just in time to catch the comprehension dawning in their eyes.

"We get enough to put in their water in the right amounts to make these folks groggy for a couple hours. Three hundred milligrams of Benadryl and an ounce of vodka per pint ought to do it."

"Miss Vicki, how'd you come to know about a thing like that?"

"I'm an editor, Happ. You pick up all kinds of esoteric knowledge. Anyway, while they're out of it, we load them on Happ's stake-body and drive them into Harrisonburg. Drop them off at the hospital, or the armory, or wherever there's still water trucks coming in. They're saved. We're saved. *And* we keep our home."

"They'll taste it," says Tom.

"Yeah, they might," Susan replies. "But then, they might just be so thirsty, they'll finish it off before they think too much about it."

"What about these kids?" Tippy asks, "Do we drug them too?"

"No need. They'll go along with their parents willingly."

Into the pause that follows, Mack says softly, "They're dying. Just outside that fence. There's people dying already. We have to try."

I see a lot of furrowed brows in the weak light from the stove. Then Tom breaks the silence.

"Well, shit. Has anybody got a better idea?"

Five of us creep quietly outside the fence and pick our way down the mountain. It's me, Susan, and Mack, because it was our idea, plus Bright and Breeze, maybe because they're young and can cover a lot of ground.

Most of the doors, we don't even have to knock on. The folks who live there have either fled for the cities or are up there at Long Man's Pillow, keeping watch over the spring. Only Althea, Ida, and a handful of others, elderly or sick, remain in town.

It's getting light by the time I meet up with the girls on the porch outside Bright's store. I show off the bottle and a half of Benadryl I scored from someone's medicine cabinet, plus some chewable tablets Althea had in a kitchen drawer.

Mack proudly shows off two bottles.

Susan has only one bottle she got from Ida. It looks dried up, but we figure we can bring it back to life with a little vinegar. "Will this be enough? There's got to be more than forty of them up there."

"We don't have to knock them out completely. Just take the legs out from under them."

Breeze and Bright emerge from the store a few moments. "Sorry for the wait, folks," Breeze says cheerily. "Store's been ransacked. Little bit of a clusterfuck in there. Nevertheless…"

He shows us four unopened bottles from the store shelves, plus a couple of backpacks crammed with tarps, duct tape, and plastic sheeting. "We can make hammocks, for carrying our guests down the mountain while they snooze. What service!" He chuckles.

We hike back up, carry our loot in plastic Christmas General Store grocery bags. It's light by the time we get back to the compound, but hopefully, with the shopping bags, we look like we've just been on a supply run.

In late afternoon, Tom, Happ, Carl, and Tippy go out to different parts of the fence and announce that the water will be dispensed in an hour. They propose to call a truce at sunset and talk things out.

The people from the Springs nod in docile agreement. Some inside this fence would say thirst has taken all the fight out of them. But there's no more desire for bloodshed in most of these folks than there is in any of us.

"People are just people," I say softly to myself. Then I snort. When did I start sounding like Alaric?

While we five were rounding up bottles of Benadryl, the folks at the spring gathered jerry cans, filled them, and tucked them out of sight, so no one outside the fence would see us adding our secret ingredient.

After it's in, and the cans are stirred, Tippy and Breeze take turns guarding the cans. They send me off to check the fences. Today there's only one spot where someone's been twisting the links open. Easy enough work to reinforce it with a little wire.

Carl has a plan to make sure no one hoards the water. Instead of giving them the cans, we're dispensing it through pipes at four different spots. Carl and Breeze round up leftover bits of PVC pipe from the construction of the reservoir and fit them through the chain-link fence and over the barbed-wire-topped walls. They prop them with forked branches so that they slope downward.

As he lifts his jerry can to the mouth of the pipe, Tippy mutters, "A toast. To Rennie."

"Shut up, Tippy," Carl growls.

The folks from the Springs crowd around the ends of the pipes, holding out cups, thermoses, milk jugs, and soda bottles. Inside the fence, we're two at each pipe: while one person steadies the raised end of the pipe, another lifts the jerry can and pours. The people from the Springs close their eyes as they drink.

Bright is in mid-pour when she suddenly drops the jerry can and races across the camp. A small boy has filled himself a tin cup of water from one of the drugged cans and is about to take a drink. "No, no, honey! That ain't for you!"

Bright knocks the cup out of his hands. The boy bursts into tears.

Susan and I exchange glances.

Piping water to all the people outside the fence takes nearly all of what's in our tiny reservoir. There's not enough left for us today. We'll let it refill overnight and drink tomorrow. It's our turn to go without.

Something about this feels right to me, righter than a hell of a lot that's been going on up here lately. A tiny ray of warmth glows in my belly, like a miniature sunrise. What's that called? It's been so long. Ah yes. That's hope.

The people from the Springs, their thirst finally sated, head off to their own makeshift camps to rest. That's a sign our cocktail is working.

Breeze and a few other folks on ATVs accompany Happ down the mountain to get his stake-body truck.

We feed the children canned peaches and pears, dinner with liquid built-in, since we can't quench their thirst until morning. I turn down the can of fruit cocktail Tom offers me. It'll only make me thirstier.

I lie back on my blankets and let the tension ease from my muscles. My mountain hasn't been this quiet since the day I arrived.

It's nearly dark when we gather up duct tape and tarps. We

want the people to stay immobilized for the whole trip, even if Bright's potion begins to wear off.

We move silently toward their tents. Susan slips inside the flap of the first one.

"Oh God. Oh shit!"

I drop what I'm doing and hurry over to her.

"They're not breathing. Shit! Vicki, they're not breathing!" Susan's cradling a woman we spoke to yesterday. Her head flops limply into Susan's lap.

I press two fingers against the side of the woman's neck. No pulse.

"Check everybody."

We go from tent to tent. Carl pulls out a plastic shaving mirror and holds it below the nostrils of the curly-haired father. Not even the slightest wisp of breath.

Susan's eyes are wide. "What the hell else was in that water?"

13

The January twilight is cold enough to bite but my insides have gone even colder.

I've already figured out where all this is headed: even if we never discover who did this horrible thing, there's a price that must be paid. Someone has to take the blame. And in a tiny close-knit rural place like Cooper's Forge, where no one leaves for generations, it's probably going to be the outsider. That girl from the city who rolled into town not even eight months ago.

I glance around the compound at my friends; all at once, they've become strangers. Would they turn on me? Do they have a choice?

"Vicki? Hey!" Susan grabs my wrist. With a tilt of her head, she indicates the huddle of children. They're awake, staring out at us silently from their mounds of blankets, as though paralyzed.

"Mack, Tippy," Susan calls out softly. "Take those kids down to Althea's."

They nod and move toward the clump of children. Good choice, those two, I think. They're parents; they'll know how to…they're parents…

"Wait!" The words fly from my mouth before my mind is done thinking them. "Tippy. You stay with us." Tippy freezes mid-stride and fixes me with a glare. "We need you," I stammer. "To help. With something here. Let Susan and Mack take the kids."

They say the closer people become, the fewer words they have to say to make themselves understood to one another. Susan, my friend of only seven months, requires no words at all from me in this moment. Everything she needs to know is in my eyes. She places a hand on Mack's shoulder and gently pats her in the direction of the kids.

I hand Tippy a roll of tarp and escort him over to the gate, where Carl and a few others are working out the logistics of burying thirty-four people. If only I could telegraph to Carl, Tom, anybody, to keep an eye on Tippy. Because I can't forget what I heard him say just before he poured the water into the pipe.

For Rennie...

Happ's stake-body truck trundles up the mountainside: life-saving transport an hour ago; now, it's a hearse.

I hurry back to the fence and discover Tom's already begun what I was going to do next. He lifts one of the jerry cans to his nose and sniffs it. He pours the dregs into a tin cup. Bits of dark leaves and seeds float on top of the water.

His eyes go wide. "Wash. Wash your hands. Don't touch anything. Go scrub the hell out of your hands."

"What? Tom, what is that shit?"

"I have my suspicions, but I don't know herbs. I know who does..."

"Who?"

"You're not gonna like it. Your geezer pal, that mountain fella. The professor."

"Alaric? Alaric's back?"

"Rumor has it. A few folks thought they seen him."

"Come on, Tom. You're not saying Alaric would murder all these people."

"He'd know just the right plant to do it. He'd know the dose. He knows how many they are. And...hold on, gal, just hear me out: he's got the motive."

"No. Not possible."

"They tried to take his spring. They killed his animals. They tried to kill *him*."

"He wouldn't."

"You think you know him, Vicki. But trust me. Ain't nobody really does."

⇢

Gertie walks behind me with her tail curled between her legs. Alaric once told me dogs hate the smell of human death more than anything else. She knows something's gone badly wrong. At any other time, a trip to Alaric's would have her wagging herself to pieces.

Alaric's carefully tended little patch of heaven looks mummified, without its animals, without any signs of the careful and deliberate life one man led there.

My breath catches in my throat. The door hangs open. Inside, a figure moves in the dim shadows.

"Alaric?"

"Vicki, honey, is that you?" Susan appears in the doorway. I nearly pee myself with relief.

"I thought you were with Mack and the kids?"

"We were on our way down to Althea's when something dawned on me. I had to come over here and check. Don't worry about the kids; Mack's got 'em to Althea's by now. But come here, look."

She gestures for me to join her inside Alaric's cabin. She points to muddy boot marks on the floor, empty cans of chili on the table, crumpled plastic moon pie wrappers. Under the chair, there's even a wadded Christmas General Store bag.

Whoever's been living in here, it sure isn't Alaric.

"There's more. Look—"

Susan leads me to Alaric's larder at the back of the cabin, where the floor goes from oak planking to bare earth. She points to a spot near the back where the dirt looks softer.

I press at the rectangle of smooth dirt with the toe of my boot. It gives, the way the rest of the ground doesn't. I kneel and dig with my fingers. The dirt comes away easily. Susan digs with me. We unearth an antique tobacco tin. Susan pulls it out of the dirt and opens the lid. She lifts out a tiny white porcelain bowl, hardly larger than an egg cup. A yellowish-brown smear of lumpy paste stains the inside of the bowl. Inside it rests an object I mistake for a white porcelain coat-peg.

"Mortar and pestle," Susan says. "Everybody knows Alaric

does weird shit with herbs. He wouldn't hide it unless…" She brings the bowl to her nose. "Oh God. Vicki. What does that smell like to you?"

I take the bowl and bring it as close to my face as I dare. "Almonds?"

"Hemlock. Oh, Jesus, it's hemlock."

❧

We tromp back to Althea's in silence. Susan won't meet my eye. It's as though a hard, heavy mass is lodged in my chest, like a dry river stone.

"It makes no sense," I say, as though each word weighs twenty pounds. "Why would he take all those pains to bring those people water, to do everything, really, absolutely every last thing he could possibly do for them. And then do that?"

"They tried to kill him, Vix. That's one good way to sour a neighborly relationship."

In Althea's living room, Becky and Cindy have draped old bedspreads over chairs and coffee tables to make a giant fort. Most of the kids from the Springs are inside it, along with most of the dogs of Cooper's Forge. Becky reads *A Wrinkle in Time* to them by flashlight. Mack snoozes in an easy chair. Althea trundles about the kitchen. Sophia, my young friend from the Springs, follows her. The two of them murmur to each other about pillows and blankets, apple juice and napkins. I can smell brownies baking.

Mack stirs as we enter. Her eyes fly open. "It's about time, you two. Come here, quick."

She pulls us over to Althea's cellar door. "Guess who Althea caught helping himself to her pantry." She picks up an iron fire poker resting against one wall, lifts the latch, and lets the door swing open. Below in the cellar, Bill Pike sits on an apple crate. He gives us a sidelong glance, flips us off with both hands, then turns his back.

Mack locks the door and turns to face us with a satisfied smirk.

"So, it was him, then," I say, slowly.

It does make sense. The people of Cooper's Forge are unanimous in this: whatever it is in human beings that makes them capable of seeing each other as more than furniture, more than objects to be tinkered with, Bill Pike just never seemed to have it. He wouldn't even need water as an excuse. He would kill all those people just to see what it was like.

My heart aches for Mack, who all this time has had to stand guard over her son's killer. But I can't help the flood of relief that washes through me, at not having to defend Alaric. The stone in my belly begins to soften.

Then Althea steps into the living room, wiping her hands on her apron. "Only one problem. I caught that little stinker two nights ago, while you all was up't the spring. Had him locked up in the cellar ever since. So, it couldn't have been him."

I'm running on adrenaline and Althea's hot black coffee. She's laced it with a little bourbon. It burns going down, warms my belly and clears my head. It's deep night, or dark morning; I've lost track of what day. A time out of time. A day and hour that have no names.

The grief-ravaged kids are asleep in the living room. Seven of us sit around in Althea's kitchen, on vinyl chairs, fold-out stools, and two of us on top of her deep freezer. Our voices float, dream-like.

We talk about what to do with Bill Pike, the kids, the bodies up on the mountain. Mostly, we try to wrap our exhausted, frozen minds around what happened that night.

Mack has convinced us Tippy never left her side that night.

"So then, Alaric. Lurking around on the mountain. Just waiting for his moment." Tom curls implicit question-marks around each of his words.

"Well, his cabin sure looked lived in."

"By Bill Pike, Susan, for God's sake." I sound harsher than I intend to.

My friend throws me a pained glance. "It doesn't mean Alaric wasn't there too, at some point."

"No. It couldn't have been him."

You don't know that," says Happ.

"It just wasn't."

"Then who?"

We probe our neighbor's faces for clues. We all seem to be having trouble meeting each other's eyes.

Sips of coffee all around. It's getting cold. Mack gets up to use the bathroom and check on the kids. Cindy, who had been asleep, tiptoes in for a drink of water, then throws her arms around my shoulders and squeezes. I pat her arm. She's wearing one of Althea's yellow housecoats as pajamas. She drifts back out to the living room.

Tom's voice breaks the silence. "So, the night the Springs folks crashed Steen's compound, the fucker—"

Althea tuts loudly.

"—took off on his quad. A couple of the younger guys chased after him. Do we actually know what they did with him?"

Happ regards his cup of bourbon-coffee as though the truth floats inside it somewhere. "All's I know is, we ain't seen him since. That don't mean he ain't up there still."

"Steen. Laying low in the woods all this time, surviving on who knows what, and then he just pops up one night to poison our water?" Susan cocks an eyebrow at him.

"I'll allow it doesn't seem likely."

"Something like fifty people around the spring that night, inside and outside the fence, and nobody saw him?"

"Well, we haven't talked to everybody, have we?"

"They's thirty-three souls that won't have a lot to say about it," Althea says.

"We could ask the children," Mack volunteers. "Tomorrow."

"We can sit down with everyone who was there that night, ask them what they remember."

We begin to tick off the names of the townsfolk in the

compound with us that night. Then, in one instant, it seems as though we all come to the same realization.

"Guys," I say softly, "when was the last time anybody saw Bright and Breeze?"

We bury the bodies in one of the swimming pools at the Springs. We place them carefully, cover them in soft black earth, then finish off with a layer of debris and leaves.

Nobody calls the police. No one's left to answer our call anyway, not in our part of the world. We've got to make our own justice, from scratch, just like we make biscuits. We do the best we can.

Bright and Breeze's brick-red camper is gone from behind the store. The place is locked, but the rickety back door gives way to a few good kicks. Inside, under a mound of plastic bags, we find an empty tin with the same yellow-brown paste Susan discovered at Alaric's.

We're a long way from healing, but we begin to thaw a little. We eat, we clean clothes, we make plans. Cindy and Beth check the weather station at the top of the hill each day. Twice a week, Carl drives up to Long Man's Pillow in the flatbed truck with the water tank and leaves it to fill overnight. Then he drives it into town. It's not exactly enough for everyone, but we make it do.

It takes us a bit longer to figure out what to do with Bill Pike and the kids. Bill will make trouble for us wherever we put him, guaranteed. So, we're not in a hurry to let him go. But these fourteen kids, every one of them traumatized and malnourished: if they have any living family anywhere in this parched and broken world, that's where they need to be.

For a few days, Gertie and I are alone on our mountain. At home, but not at peace. In that grounded silence, where birds pass the news of the day from ridge to ridge and the hours unwind with the moving of the light through the trees, in the one place I've ever been that feels as though I belong, I come to understand what I must do next.

I ask the townsfolk to give me a few more days, alone.

The first thing I do is wrap up all the barbed wire into a tight coil. I drag it to the cliff edge and drop it off the mountain. Next, I borrow a heavy pair of bolt cutters from Happ and clip the chain-link fence free from its poles. I cut it into small sections to make it light enough to drag. I roll up the pieces and wrestle each one to the cliff. I kick them over the edge, one by one. Then I take down the barrier wall, car part by car part, cinderblock by cinderblock.

I make a trek up to Steen's abandoned stucco man-spread. Predictably, it's been looted. It looks partied-in. But that doesn't matter. What I'm after is still intact.

I figure out a method for prying loose the half-tube-shaped terra cotta tiles that line the roof of the house. A wheelbarrow in one of the sheds works for transporting them. I lay them, open-side-up and end to end, in a zigzag pattern, down the side of the mountain.

I dig a shallow trench beside the tiles and snug them into it to make a long chute. I cover the chute loosely with open-side-down tiles to form a kind of pipe. The last hundred feet or so, I build a raised platform out of cinderblocks for the pipe to ride on, ending in the main pool of Kelso Springs.

I help myself to bags of concrete from the Bright Christmas General Store, which has now become a free pantry for all the town's needs, open twenty-four-seven.

I clean the debris out of the main pool and patch its cracks.

Back at the spring, I fashion a kind of sluice gate out of the fender of a Volkswagen Beetle. I wait until Carl has filled his truck and the reservoir is low. Then I take a pickaxe and chip a half-circle into the wall of the reservoir, honing it until it's just exactly the shape of a Beetle fender. I drop the fender into place and wait for the reservoir to fill again.

When it does, I lift the sluice gate, just a couple inches. Water streams into the terra-cotta chute and races down the mountain.

It takes four days to fill the pool at Kelso Springs.

The next time Carl trundles up in his flatbed to fill the water tank, I tell him to go back down the mountain and get everyone to meet me there.

❧

They arrive, one by one, two by two, in their pickups, on ATVs and dirt bikes. They stare, gape-mouthed, at the full pool and the water pouring into it.

"Hell, we're going to have to put a roof on that," says Happ.

"No roof," I say. "Put a tarp if you have to, keep leaves and dirt out. But that's all."

"How we supposed to protect that?" Tom grumbles, "It's only a matter of time till the next mob shows up."

"Ain't hardly enough for the people who live here as it is," says Carl. "That water won't hold out forever."

"Vicki, why in hell didn't you talk to us before you went and did all this?"

"That's right. You wouldn't have had no spring at all if it weren't for us."

I look at them and sigh. "Guys. Haven't we done that one already?"

They walk around, examining my handiwork. Most of them don't get it. I knew they wouldn't.

I wait until they've grumbled themselves into silence. Then I begin.

"I have no illusion that this is *my* water. But I took a long, hard look at what we became when we decided to deny it to those people, and I didn't like what I saw."

I pause and study my friends' faces. I see bewilderment, mostly. A few angry scowls. Several of the townsfolk keep their heads bowed, their expressions unreadable. But Susan and Tom, at least, are nodding solemnly. I take a breath and continue.

"You keep looking at me like I should have an answer for all this. Believe me, I don't. But the thing is, if surviving means looking another human being in the eye and calling them the enemy, just because they need the same things we need, then what's it all for? I don't want to die a minute sooner than I have to, but whenever that time comes, I want to go out with my humanity intact."

A few of the folks raise their heads and furrow their brows at me. This is getting painful.

"Now, you all can close off this pipe and put that fence back around that spring in less than a day, if that's what you want, but…" I search for a way to bring my sermon to a close. "But I'd really, really like you to be with me on this. And if you're not, well, I guess that'll have to be okay…"

By the expressions on their faces, you'd think they'd just been beaten. They shuffle from foot to foot. Then someone claps a hand on my shoulder. It's Carl. Others follow: Happ, Tippy, Tom. Susan wraps me in a fierce hug.

It's not the whole town, by any means. Quite a few are standing back from the crowd with their arms crossed, scowling. But I got through to some. To some of them, by God, I got through.

"Now all that's left is to take care of these kids. And Pike. Anybody want to give me a hand?"

Happ and Carl bind Bill Pike's hands and feet and place duct tape over his mouth. Then they plop him into Happ's flatbed and drive off into the night. They'll take him to the outskirts of Shepherdstown and leave him someplace where he'll be found, but not too soon.

Susan, Mack, and I bundle the kids from the Springs into three vehicles. I expect a flood of questions, or accusations. But they sit in silence the whole way.

When we reach Harrisonburg, it's nearly dawn. We pull over half a block from the hospital. We wake the children and give them a drink and a snack. We set them all on the sidewalk and point out the hospital entrance. The copper-haired girl hugs Gertie tightly and cries into her rumpled neck. The troop of children head toward the brightly lit doorway. We will ourselves to get back in our cars and drive like hell.

෫

When we get back to Cooper's Forge, we trundle down into the church basement. Susan and Mack make a batch of coffee, but it sits stewing in its pot, un-tasted. I rise and face the townsfolk.

"Well. I'm sure you've all figured out what's going to happen next. Either Bill Pike or one of the kids will mention what happened here. Law enforcement of one kind or another will come along asking questions."

I pause. Solemn nods all around.

"Someone's got to take the blame. Bright's family's practically an institution in this area. I don't think the heat's going to die down by blaming her. But there's this newcomer, this stranger from Baltimore."

"No, ma'am," Happ says sternly. "You ain't going to jail on our behalf; how'd we live with ourselves?"

"Oh," Mack whispers. "She ain't talking about going to jail. She's fixing to leave us."

"No. Out of the question." Tom rises from his chair. "She stays. We face this together."

Susan, my gentle, sweet friend, takes her husband by the arm and tugs him back into his seat. "Honey, I don't think any of us have a say in the matter. You know what it's like when Vicki Truax makes up her mind."

"So," I say to my neighbors, "can somebody run me up to my cabin and then come get me in a couple hours?"

I've got so much to do.

෫

Gertie and I crisscross our land, clipping and winding up string, dumping my pipe-and-bolt alarm system into a plastic garbage sack. People can come onto my land at will now.

We visit each special place to tell it goodbye. Picnic Rock. Black Drum Stump. Rennie's Kayak Tree. Gertie's bone garden. The place where I met the bear. The spot where I dug sassafras with Alaric. The familiar landmarks are still there, though they've all gone strange.

I reach the cliff-edge where I fell, that first day on my land. This time, my feet have learned how to read what's under them, and I know precisely how far out I can step without the ground giving way. I lean out, daring myself to peer into the fallen water tower.

Something's inside it. A sprawled, broken human figure, stiff, unmoving. A pool of dried black blood around it. A red and white polo shirt. An ingenious place, really, for the people from the Springs to dump Steen when they were done with him.

There's no greater measure of just how much my heart has changed, that I turn away and leave him there, where I first met him, without the slightest flicker of remorse.

14

I'm tramping back up the trail when I hear the rhythm of a hammer. It echoes from tree to tree. I'm certain it's coming from my cabin.

Gertie dashes ahead of me, yodeling joyfully.

I come within sight of the cabin. Alaric is on my roof with a mouthful of nails, hammering in a row of fresh red cedar shingles.

"What do you think you're doing?"

He looks at me over the top of his glasses. "Winter's coming. You want that cold wind slipping in between these cracks?"

I join him on my roof.

He says, "How did my goats taste?"

"I didn't eat your goats, Alaric."

"They didn't eat themselves."

"Bill Pike. He might have eaten them. We think he holed up in your cabin for a while."

"That'd explain why it smelled like moon pies."

"But it was Bright, Breeze's wife, that got into your…poison."

Alaric nods. "Cooper's Forge's own resident xenophobe. Fear of the Other: the oldest, and most destructive force in human history."

I glance at him sideways, hoping he'll answer my question without my having to ask it. For once, he does.

"I don't keep guns, city girl. No more than you do. But we're in the Appalachians. There's no vet clinic just around the corner. When one of my animals gets snake bit or breaks a leg, I have to have a fast way to tell them goodnight. Hemlock is what you keep on hand when you live in the woods, and you care about your animals."

We shingle together in silence. When we're done, Alaric says, "You should have finished this a month ago."

Every moment I linger here is a risk, but I decide another hour is worth it. I invite him in for tea. He moves stiffly, but otherwise seems to have made a full recovery. I tell him everything that's happened, from the day the people in Kelso Springs attacked him to this morning. He listens. Sometimes he nods. When I get to the parts where people die, I weep. He doesn't weep with me, but he sits in silent witness to my grief, taking it deep within himself.

We talk the afternoon away. When I've talked myself out and wept myself dry, I say, "Well, now that we've got my shingles done, why don't we go make a start on yours?"

"No need. I'm not going back to that cabin. I'm living with my daughter in Saint Paul."

"You do have a daughter?"

"Of course I have a daughter!" Alaric barks. "She's the source of all my good fortune. My water goddess." He winks at me. "My *jengu*."

A laugh escapes me. The first in a long time.

An ATV approaches the cabin and pulls up idling outside. The driver blips its horn.

"My ride," Alaric says, rising with difficulty. I open the cabin door for him. On his way out, he says, "You have the heart of a true human being, city girl. A rare thing these days."

He walks carefully onto the porch, grasps the railing, and takes each step gingerly. How he got up on my roof, I'll never know.

Then he walks to where a tall, yellow-haired woman waits on an ATV. She waves to me and smiles warmly. Alaric swings a leg over the machine and they're off, down the mountain.

I lie down on what's left of Aunt Colleen's rope bed. Gertie hops up to join me, but her paws slip between the ropes, so she contents herself with curling up for a snooze on the floor.

I gaze up into the rafters, like I used to. The creatures I shared this cabin with have moved on to their winter quarters. Or to wherever there's water. No ants march across the bark of the logs. No snakes poke their heads out of the rafters to glare at me with gleaming black eyes. No more mice come to bless my home with their litters of naked pink babies.

I drift off, pretending my little mountain home is still as I found it. Or better, as it was before I ever arrived, before the rain stopped, when my mountain stood proudly at the head of a rushing river, twisting its way to the sea, the shaggy green pillow of a long, long man.

The gnatty buzzing of an ATV engine jangles me awake. Gertie barks once, then she's all wags. I look outside the window. Susan pulls up in my yard. "It's time, honey."

My last sight of my little cabin in the woods is the same as my first: from the back of an ATV bumping along the wooded mountain track.

∂°

At the base of the mountain, Susan turns left instead of right, and takes us out of town to the car graveyard where we scavenged parts to build our wall. My crappy little green Chevy is there, engine idling. So are Carl, Tom, Happ, Mack, Tippy, and the girls, Althea, and half the town.

Hugs all around. Sniffles. Happ blushes in my arms. Becky and Cindy embrace me, then cling to each other.

Susan says, "We'll do what you said, girlfriend. We're gonna keep that spring open to all comers. We'll even keep that godawful name, The Long—what—Long Pillow?" She hugs me, then pulls away tearfully. "You won't forget us, now, will you?"

Althea leans patiently on her cane, at the end of the row of townsfolk, watching my goodbyes with her usual unreadable expression. When at last I stand before her, she studies me a moment in silence, much as she did on the first day we met. Then she says, "Your momma was a right sweet lady. I only met her the once. She brought you here when you was just a tiny thing 'cause she wanted us to know about you."

Althea purses her lips, as though she's about to say something unpleasant.

"That fella your momma made you with. Colleen's nephew. He never set one foot in this town as far as I recollect. He got himself killed before you was even knee-high and ain't a single one of us was surprised when we heard the news." Her scowl melts away and the corners of her mouth rise. "But from that day we first set eyes on you, you've been one of our own."

Althea cups my face in her two knobby hands and looks into my eyes. "You turn't out to be a damn fine mountain woman. Colleen's smiling down on you from wherever she's at."

She pats my cheek.

I told Thora I was bringing someone with me. I didn't say much more than that. She's not a fan of dogs, but she'll take us both in. I'll explain once we're there.

Not long ago, I'd never owned anything that mattered. For a tiny scrap of time, I believed I owned a chunk of land on a West Virginia mountain. Since then, I have a far different understanding of what I can and can't own. Now I'm back to having nothing again.

Not nothing. I do have a dog. And she has me.

A dog doesn't last as long as a mountain. But then, neither does a human being.

I also discovered something I've had all along: the soul of a teacher. For however long I'm alive, if I can teach, I can be useful.

Toronto is one of the last remaining cities in North America where life continues as it once did. For now.

I had thought my life on Delaney Street was normal. Yet, when I had the chance to view it through a longer lens, I found it was anything but. Except for the tiny blip on the radar screen that is civilization, we have always arranged our lives around our quest for water. We used to tell ourselves stories about the calamities that would befall us if we ever took it for granted.

That's as good a way as any to think about what has happened to us: we stopped listening to the wisdom of our own stories.

I roll down the passenger-side window and Gertie hangs her head out. I ease the old green Chevy onto the road and we begin the long climb uphill, out of Cooper's Forge, then northward.

We're going to the waters, as all our kind must do.

ACKNOWLEDGMENTS

My sincerest thanks to Jaynie Royal, Pam Van Dyk, and all the magnificent folks at Regal House Publishing.